The Planting Season

**Center Point
Large Print**

**This Large Print Book carries the
Seal of Approval of N.A.V.H.**

The Planting Season

Dorothy Garlock

CENTER POINT PUBLISHING
THORNDIKE, MAINE

This Center Point Large Print edition
is published in the year 2008 by arrangement with
Hachette Book Group USA.

The text of this Large Print edition is unabridged. In other
aspects, this book may vary from the original edition.
Printed in the United States of America.
Set in 16-point Times New Roman type.

ISBN: 978-1-60285-259-4

Library of Congress Cataloging-in-Publication Data

Garlock, Dorothy.
    The planting season / Dorothy Garlock.--Center Point large print ed.
        p. cm.
    ISBN: 978-1-60285-259-4 (lib. bdg. : alk. paper)
    1. Large type books. I. Title.

PS3557.A71645P59 2008
813'.54--dc22

2008013532

One

"Oh, for cryin' out loud! Damn that man! He's out there again."

"He is? Let me see! Ohhhh . . ." The high-pitched squeal of the teenager caused the shaggy brown dog to lift his jowls off the floor, cock his head, point his ears, and let out a husky sound between a bark and a growl.

"Lay right there and bark, you worthless hound. You wouldn't get up and bite anyone if he was carrying off everything in this house." The tall blond woman's hair swept straight back from her forehead and hung down her back in a single thick braid.

"Where, Iris? What's he doing? Ah . . . Oooh . . . look at that red hair!"

"Get away from the window, Brenda," Iris said sharply. You'll get nail polish on the drapes," she finished lamely.

"That ain't it, and you know it. You just don't want him to see us looking."

"Don't say ain't." Iris stomped across the room and flung herself down in a chair. The stuffing was beginning to show on the padded arm, and she carefully straightened the crocheted doily she had pinned there to cover it. "That . . . bastard has gone to the zoning commission, sure as hell!"

"Don't swear! You won't let me."

"You're fourteen and I'm thirty. That should give

me a license to swear if I want to," she said crossly.

"You're thirty-two, Iris. I can count. And I'm almost fifteen." Brenda sat down cross-legged on the floor beside the dog and shook the bottle of nail enamel.

"You're just what I need today, snippy little sister. You spill that polish on the carpet and you'll wish this *old* woman were in East Siberia."

"You don't have to be an old maid. You could have married Stanley."

"Oh, for heaven's sake! There's no such thing as an old maid in this day and age. And don't start on Stanley. I've got enough on my mind without your bringing up that creep." Iris stretched her denim-clad legs out in front of her and crossed her booted ankles. She reached behind her and pulled the long, thick braid over her shoulder before she rested her head against the back of the chair and folded her arms over her chest. "And please be quiet. I've got to think."

"You've been thinking for a couple of months," Brenda grumbled. "A few more minutes of thinking won't change a thing."

"I was depending on that wishy-washy zoning commission to keep that trailer out of my grove."

"It's not a trailer, it's a mobile home. And it isn't your grove." Brenda blew on the blood-red polish she had applied to her nails.

"Enjoy those claws while you can, my girl. It's almost planting season, and you're bound to lose those nails when your pretty little hands are glued to the steering wheel of the tractor every minute you're out of school."

"What's *he* going to do? I thought he was coming out here to learn to be a farmer. How is he going to learn anything if I do all the work?" Brenda capped the polish bottle, and rolled over onto her stomach so she could get a better look at her scowling sister.

Iris had always looked younger than her age until recently. Now the signs of her years of struggle to farm the land and supply a stable, comfortable home for her sister were beginning to show. Faint lines of strain had appeared lately between her brows and at the corners of her eyes and mouth. Her sun-tanned face often had a pensive look, with shadows of worry beneath her eyes.

Iris's wide mouth, its lower lip fuller and softer than the upper one, turned down at the corner, reflecting her less-than-happy mood. Her blond hair was her most startling feature, but her eyes ran a close second. They were wide and blue-gray, deep-set, and tilted at the outer corners, under well-defined brows only a shade darker than her hair. They glared now at the young girl who was more like a daughter than a sister.

"You know I don't like for you to bring that dog into the living room," she said irritably. "He gets hair and mud and Lord knows what else all over the carpet."

"Just cause you're mad and can't do anything about *him,* you're taking your spite out on Arthur." Brenda rolled onto her back and scratched the dog's shaggy head. "Ain't that right, Arthur?"

"Don't say ain't."

Brenda sighed heavily. "I *haven't* been able to see him up close. Do you think he'll come to the house?"

"I sure as hell hope not!"

"Don't swear." With the quickness of youth, Brenda flipped up onto her knees so she could rest her chin on Iris's slim thigh. "It isn't so bad, Iris. He could have moved into the house, you know."

"Over my dead body!"

Brenda looked up with a sympathetic smile. "Couldn't you vamp him?"

"Vamp him? You've lost your marbles!" Iris got to her feet and stood with her hands on her hips, looking down at the younger girl. Brenda was long-limbed and slightly gawky, due to her height. Her nose, lightly dusted with freckles, turned up pertly, giving her face a pixieish look. Her hair was several shades darker than her sister's, and parted in the back, with bunches tied with ribbon hanging over each shoulder.

"Dad should have had his head examined for taking old Mrs. Lang on as a partner," Iris said. "I tried to get him to go to the bank, but he was bound and determined to sell half the farm to her. He must have thought she would die before he did and would leave it to him in her will." Iris began to walk up and down the room, paused to move the curtain aside so she could peek out toward the grove, snorted, and let the curtain fall back in place. "That fool is out there stepping off the place where he's going to put that rolling shoe box!"

"I don't think anyone knew old Mrs. Lang had a grandson in the Navy. She used to talk about Junior. It was Junior this and Junior that. I thought she was just making it up."

"Well, she wasn't. John D. Lang, Jr. is living proof."

"I thought only really old men retired, Iris. Does he have to work?"

"I don't know about that. The lawyer told me that he went into the Navy when he was eighteen and retired after twenty years of service," Iris said drily.

"Then he's not young! Oh, shoot! He's old. Thirty-eight . . . *wow!*"

Iris raised her eyes to the ceiling. "Yeah. He's practically got one foot in the grave."

"That's for sure! And he's too old to learn to farm. Maybe he likes you, Iris. He wouldn't be too old for *you.*"

"Thanks a lot." Iris turned her head away, hiding her face, suddenly contorted with the pain of remembering her forty-five-year-old father bringing home a bride less than half his age. A year later, the year she graduated from high school, Brenda was born. A year after that the young bride took off for parts unknown, disillusioned with being married to an old man who didn't have the money she thought he had. During Iris's college years her father hired a woman to care for Brenda, but since then it had been she alone who'd raised her halfsister.

"Arrr-woof!" Arthur got lazily to his feet and started for the kitchen door.

"You may be a pussycat, Arthur, but you've got super ears." Brenda shot a guarded look at her sister. "He's coming to the house. What are you gonna do?"

"Meet him outside." Iris stomped through the dining room to the kitchen, grabbed a worn denim jacket hanging on a straight-backed chair, and jerked it on over her hooded sweatshirt. She stood on the back steps, digging the hood out from under the back of her jacket, and watched the source of her irritation come toward her.

He was a bear of a man. His height topped her five-foot ten-inch frame by half a foot. Broad in the shoulders and chest, yet solid and lean through the waist and hips, he had long, well-muscled legs and walked with a rolling gait. His easy stride brought him quickly across the graveled drive, past the black iron water pump set on a concrete slab, and through the swinging gate.

Iris stood stock still, head tilted back, arms folded. She stared in mixed exasperation and desperation, her smoky eyes analytical as they moved over his strong neck, not exactly handsome face, and the shock of brick-red hair. She remembered his face as being harsher when she'd voiced her disapproval after he'd calmly announced his intention to participate actively in the operation of the farm. They had been sitting in the lawyer's office, and Iris had declared in no uncertain terms she thought it stupid—no, downright asinine—for him to assume he could be any practical help on the farm.

The only other time they had met was when she stood on the steps, as she was doing now, and told him she was not going to permit him to move "a long, skinny boxcar of a thing" onto her homestead, and if the prefabricated dwelling had any place at all in the scheme of things it was in a trailer park in town, and not out here.

Iris was slightly breathless with anger as she shifted her gaze from his face to the figure of the zoning commissioner, who was getting into his car, and then back to his face. Smile lines bracketed his wide mouth; his thick red hair looked as if he'd been in a windstorm, and it glistened in the sun; his brilliant, pure blue eyes glinted as he assessed her stance. He was pleased with himself, Iris realized, and she was filled with even more resentment.

"The commissioner says there's nothing in the county ordinance to prevent me from putting the mobile home right out there." John waved his hand toward the grove of pine and spruce trees that had been planted by her grandfather as a windbreak when he'd built the house eighty years before.

Iris stiffened visibly but didn't speak. His heavy, brown brows lowered in a frown as he noticed her reaction. Before he could speak again the screen door opened behind Iris and nudged her aside so Brenda and Arthur could come out.

"Hi."

"Hi. You must be Brenda Ouverson."

"In living color. You must be Junior. Come here,

Arthur. That's rude!" She grabbed the dog's collar and pulled him back. "He has to check out everything and everybody that comes on this place," she said with an apologetic grin. "He'll get used to you, but I doubt if Iris will."

"Knock it off, Brenda," Iris said sharply.

"I'm afraid Miss Ouverson will have to get used to me or else sell me her part of the farm." He spoke to Brenda, but his narrowed gaze was on Iris.

"Call her Iris, Junior. Kids at school call her Miss Ouverson when she subs, but nobody else does."

"My name's John." He bent down to rub the dog behind the ears with long, strong fingers. "The plumber will be out tomorrow to run the gas and water lines. It will be simpler if they tie onto your meters and we share the expense."

A quick, nervous spate of words broke from Iris's tight lips. "Why are you so determined to bring that thing out here? This homestead is eighty years old. My father made every effort to preserve its character, and so will I. The barns are old, but they've been maintained beautifully through the years, with an eye to keeping the original design of the buildings. This homestead is graced with an air of dignity and a sense of permanence. You roll that pencil box in here and you'll not only ruin that grove, but you'll create an eyesore the whole county will be talking about."

"You know the alternative," he said softly.

"You know damn well it's unthinkable for you to move into the house with us."

12

"Everything is thinkable," he corrected with a rueful grin. "But I expect it *would* give the conservative Iowans in town something interesting to gossip about."

"You mean they'd think you were sleeping with Iris? Ha! Fat chance! She won't even kiss Stanley." Brenda nonchalantly swung her leg over Arthur to hold him between her knees while she looked critically at her polished nails.

Iris was almost giddy with embarrassment. Her eyes glittered with both anger and despair, and she turned the full force of them on her sister. "That's enough out of you, Brenda. You've got chores."

"Okay, okay," Brenda said with a lift of her shoulders. "Just don't get your motor all revved up over nothing."

John reached out a big hand and clapped it over the top of her head and gave it a friendly shake. Brenda was not as tall as her sister, but she was equally as thin and willowy. Her legs seemed endless in the tight jeans; beneath the heavy turtleneck sweater she wore there was a hint of small, nicely rounded breasts and a wispy waist.

"See ya." Blue eyes in a pert face darted a look at him. "It's get rid of Brenda time. My sister probably wants to swear at you, and she thinks I've never heard a swear word before. C'mon, Arthur. Let's head for the barn and Dullsville."

John watched her lope away, the dog at her heels. He turned back to the grim-faced woman on the steps. "How old is she?"

13

"Fourteen, and out of bounds for you," Iris snapped.

"Oh, for the Lord's sake!" He stifled an oath, then spun on his heel to walk away, but turned back with an angry scowl on his face. He pointed his finger at her. "Listen. I could have forced you to sell out to me, as long as I offered to buy your part of this farm and you couldn't raise the money to buy me out. Partnerships work that way, in case you didn't know or have forgotten. I realize this farm has been in your family since its existence, and therefore I'm willing to share it with you—at least until your sister is out of school and on her own. That assumes, of course, we can last that long without killing each other. Now, it can be a pleasant business arrangement or it can be a battle every step of the way." He snapped his teeth together, straightened to his full height and rocked back on his heels. "I didn't spend twenty years in the Navy for nothing. I don't give up easily. I fight for what I want, and I want to live here on this home-stead and farm the land my grandmother bought for me."

The stress lines between Iris's brows deepened, and her mouth tensed. "In other words take you and your *cracker box* or sell out to you, at your price, and move on. Is that it?"

"Exactly."

Iris pushed her hands into her pockets and hunched her shoulders. "You've played all the right cards. Or rather your grandmother played them for you."

He shrugged. "Either way, I'm here and I'm staying.

14

I'll be out in the morning with the plumbers. A few days after that I'll bring in the house."

Iris pressed her lips together tightly and half turned, so he couldn't see the tears that glistened on her thick lashes. The tension that had been building in her for days had mounted to produce a splitting headache: all she wanted to do at this moment was slip inside that screened door, hide in the house, and cry. But damned if she would! She wouldn't retreat with her tail between her legs. She'd brazen it out, even if it killed her!

"Iris!" Brenda called from the barn door. "Where's that plastic bucket I use to feed the calf?"

"In the machine shed, where you left it." Iris lifted the heavy braid of hair off her chest and flung it over her shoulder. She looked directly at John D. Lang, Jr. for a full ten seconds before she spoke. "You win, Mr. Lang. But I don't have to like it." She forced herself to concentrate on keeping her poise, her tears at bay, her fists from flying out to hit him, while fantasizing about his disappearing beneath the manure spreader.

John backed off a few steps, hesitated, then said, "The mobile home won't stick out like a sore thumb regardless of what you think. After I finish with it, it'll blend into the surroundings. I plan to add a screened porch across the front to break the straight line and have the whole thing painted to match the trim of this house."

"Oh, great! That should be just dandy. A white house, a green house, a red barn. Christmas all year

15

long," Iris said with a stoical calmness she didn't feel at all. She was pleased to see the flicker of annoyance on John's face.

He half turned so he could look toward the grove. "I'll have the house set in the long way, then the front will face the drive. When I add the porch and the carport, I may have to take out one small tree."

"Noooooo! You're not cutting down my trees!" A pounding began in Iris's head that threatened to make her eyes go out of focus. Since her father's death, five years ago, she had been in charge here, and had guarded every tree as if it were the last one on earth. *No, sir! This sailor wasn't going to cut down a single one of her trees!*

"The grove needs to be thinned. For now I'll only take out the tree with the NO HUNTING sign on it."

"You'll do no such thing! What in the hell did you learn in the Navy that makes you so all-fired smart about thinning a grove?" Chin up, body taut, Iris was mindful of the thudding in her chest, the pounding in her head. Mustering the fragments of her self-possession, she locked her gaze to his and refused to look away.

His eyes were cobalt-blue and fenced with thick brown lashes, topped by reddish-brown brows, which were now drawn together with displeasure. As she watched, his features formed a deeper frown, the muscle in one lean cheek jumping in response to his clenched teeth. His gaze fell from her eyes to the soft and vulnerable curve of her lips, lingered long enough

16

to send an unwelcome tremor through her, and then passed down to the arms folded tightly across her chest. He made no attempt to conceal his impatience with her. The pounding in Iris's head expanded into her stomach and echoed through that empty chamber.

He spread his long, denim-clad legs and hooked his hands in his hip pockets. The movement spread his jacket and revealed an open-neck knit shirt with a small monogrammed symbol on the chest. Iris's eyes flicked to his feet and the blue-and-gray sneakers. A stray thought passed quickly through her mind. Nikes! Good heavens. Who would have guessed they made them that big?

"So this is the way it's going to be, huh?" John said thoughtfully. "You're going to drag your feet every step of the way."

"If necessary." Iris wanted to scream. More than that, she wanted to hit something—preferably him.

"I've had young kids come into the Navy with chips on their shoulders. Some thought they knew it all. You can bet they were whipped into line before they shipped out." His brows lifted in a silent message.

"I'm no kid, Mr. Lang, and this isn't the Navy. You're in my territory. We'll see who is whipped into line." Her voice was low, with the force of her anger held in check.

"I-r-is! Where's the pine tar? Candy's got a cut on her fetlock."

"On the shelf in the tack house," she called, grateful for the interruption. Casually, with an outward calm

17

belying both the ache behind her forehead and the dancing devils in her stomach, she began to walk toward the barn. Leaving the *sailor* standing on the walk, she thought that surely he'd have the good manners to leave. Not true. He appeared beside her, matching his stride to hers.

"Who's Candy?"

"Sugar's colt."

"There aren't any horses listed in the farm inventory."

She stopped and turned on him like a spitting cat. "Sugar and the colt belong to Brenda. She bought the mare with money she earned, and she paid the stud fee. There are two more horses on this farm that have never been listed. They belong to me."

"I see," he said—to her back, because she had walked away.

Iris pulled back the bottom half of the barn door, latched it to the top half, stepped over the thick doorsill, and into the barn. A single light burned at the end of the row of stalls. For once Brenda hadn't turned on every light in the barn. They had been trying to lower their huge electric bills.

Attempting to ignore John D. Lang, Jr., who was trailing close behind her—and her throbbing head— Iris kicked at the clean straw with her booted feet as she went down the narrow passage. A devilish hope that he'd step in some manure and soil his spotless Nikes briefly crossed her mind.

Brenda was waiting beside a tan-and-white-spotted

colt, holding the rope halter and rubbing the soft nose that nuzzled her arm. "I didn't notice it until she followed Sugar in and I saw the blood," she wailed. "There must be some barbed wire down somewhere."

Iris knelt down beside the colt, rubbing her hand up and down the slender leg, keeping well back in case the sharp little hoof lashed out. "Did you get the pine tar?"

"I didn't want to turn her loose. Is it bad? It bled a lot."

"I'll get the tar. Where is it?" The masculine voice came from far above Iris's head.

She stood and gave him a disgusted look. "You wouldn't know pine tar from . . . apple butter," she said, and stomped off down the aisle.

"I don't think she likes you, Junior." Brenda's blue eyes had to look up a long way to reach his face.

"I think you're right."

"She's gettin' one of her headaches. It's been coming on all day. By night she'll be throwing up her socks."

"She suffers from migraines?"

"Yeah. I think that's what she calls them. You're enough to give even me a headache, Junior."

"My name's John."

"Then why was ol' Mrs. Lang always callin' you Junior?"

"Reasonable question." He reached out and fondled the colt's ears. The animal tossed her head.

"Horses don't like to have their ears touched," Brenda said quickly.

19

"Oh? Sorry. Back to why my grandmother called me Junior. I don't think she realized I had grown up. I was away at sea most of the time, and my trips home were few and far between. Granny sometimes thought I was my dad. How old is the colt?"

"A month. Do you like horses?"

"I like 'em, but I don't know much about 'em."

"I could teach you that. Sugar was my 4-H project a few years ago. She got a blue ribbon at the fair. Hey, we're looking for a new leader. Want to be one?"

"What in the heck would he know about being a 4-H leader?" Iris walked into the stall with a can and paddle in one hand and a roll of paper towels in the other. She knelt down, pried off the lid, and dipped the clean wooden paddle into the thick black tar. "Whoa, girl. Easy, now. This will make it feel better, and keep the flies off, too." Talking to the colt in a calm, smooth voice all the while she dabbed the medicine on the cut, Iris concluded, "That should do it." She wiped the stick clean on the paper towel and replaced the lid on the can. "Put her back in the stall so Sugar can see what we've done to her baby," she said as she stepped up onto the bottom board of the stall to reach the nose of the brown-and-black-spotted mare. She gave her a gentle pat; then the horse's pointed ears stood at attention when Iris brought a handful of molasses-soaked grain and pellets out of her pocket and held it to the soft lips, which quickly began to nibble. "You like that, don't you, girl?" she crooned softly to the horse, and placed a kiss on her nose.

When Iris stepped down too quickly from the rail, a jarring pain coursed through her head; it was followed by a quick succession of pains so sharp that she almost swayed. "Finish up here, will you, Brenda? Feed Buck and Boots for me tonight. I'm going to the house."

"Will you be too sick to take me to town later?" Brenda called as she reached the door.

"Of course not!" she said as confidently as she could manage.

"Do you have migraines often?" John asked while she was closing the bottom half of the barn door.

"No! You're the only big headache I've had in a long time." Iris gritted her teeth.

He ignored her sarcasm. "What do you take for it?"

"Aspirin, aspirin, and aspirin. You caused it," she blurted. "When you leave it'll probably go with you." Ignoring him now, she concentrated only on breathing deeply to keep her stomach from heaving, and on placing one foot in front of the other so she could get to the house. She reached the screen door and flung it open: "Goodbye, so long, happy sailing," she muttered, and stumbled into the house.

She dropped her jacket on the kitchen floor, jerked her boots off with the bootjack, and reeled to the newel post at the foot of the stairs. She leaned on the rounded top, hoping the demons pounding in her head would let up long enough for her to make it up the steps. Her stomach convulsed, and she groaned.

"Iris, let me help you."

Him again! It was too much. She closed her eyes

21

tightly and held onto the post, knowing that any minute she was going to further humiliate herself with a crying jag. Everything hurt so damn bad!

"What have I done to deserve you?" she croaked feebly. This was the enemy, but strangely, she couldn't fight any longer. An arm slid across her back, and she was pulled against a broad chest. Too sick to reject this gesture of help, Iris leaned into the arms that steadied her and the long, warm body that absorbed the tremors that shook her. Reeling and desperately afraid she would throw up, she let him help her up the stairs.

"The bathroom . . ." She staggered away from him and through the open door, not even bothering to close it, and sank down on the edge of the tub. Holding the blond braid in her hand, she leaned over the stool as the bathroom door closed, allowing her to lose the contents of her stomach in private.

Her migraine had reached gigantic proportions by the time she wet a cloth and grabbed a bottle of aspirin from the medicine cabinet. John was waiting outside the door. His identity was no longer important to Iris. He was help. She headed down the hall to her bed-room with his hand beneath her arm to steady her. Somehow they both made it through the narrow door and to the soft bed. She buried her face in the pillow to shut out the light. Her senses were so numbed by pain that she was only vaguely aware that she was between the cool sheets and the covers were being pulled up around her neck.

At that moment Iris didn't care if it was John D. Lang, Jr. or Adolph Hitler in her bedroom pulling the window shades. She welcomed the darkness. Her mind was a jungle; her stomach an ocean in which nausea kept coming and going in waves. Somewhere along the way she had dropped the wet cloth, but the aspirin bottle was still clutched in her hand. Warm, strong fingers pried hers loose from the bottle. She let go. Nothing mattered but to be left alone.

It wasn't to be. He was back.

"Take this aspirin, Iris." He put tablets in her mouth. She tried to push him away. His arm lifted and turned her, and he held a glass to her lips. Wincing, she swallowed the tablets and a sip of water. He eased her back down on the bed and covered her again.

Later, somewhere in the sea of agony that held her, she felt a warm hand on her forehead, strong fingers gently stroking her temples, soothing away the pain, and at last she fell into a deep dreamless sleep.

Two

Groggy, Iris pushed up onto a bent elbow, blinked, and swept the hair back from her eyes so she could see the digital clock. The red numbers swam before her eyes, and she squinted to hold them in place. Nine-thirty? She had slept for five hours? Moving slowly, she threw back the covers and sat up on the side of the bed. The ghost of the headache was still there, but she felt vastly improved. Shaking off the fogginess, she flipped on the bedside lamp, and the room was flooded with a soft glow.

A glass of water and the aspirin bottle sat on the nightstand—along with a new, dark plastic bottle with a prescription label. Iris reached for it, a quizzical frown on her face. Her doctor's name was typed neatly above hers on the label and beneath were the directions for taking the capsules. The prescription had been filled at Casey Rexal Drug, her pharmacy. A misty memory came to mind of being lifted, of something being put into her mouth, of a masculine voice telling her to swallow. Glory! Was she so freaked out from the headache that she took just any medication, like a slave on command?

Iris got to her feet, went to the bathroom, and washed her face. Thank God the nausea was gone. She felt decidedly better. She had to see what Brenda was up to. Longtime habits of concern were hard to forget.

Halfway down the stairs the aroma of freshly brewed coffee caused her bare feet to pause for an instant before they continued on down the steps. Iris swung around the newel post at the same time that her eyes swung about the room. One small lamp burned. The television screen was dark. Strange. Brenda thought the house would cave in if the set wasn't turned on. A stab of uneasiness struck her, and she hurried to the lighted kitchen. Surprise brought her to a halt in the doorway.

John Lang sat at her kitchen table, a cup of coffee at hand. Scattered over the table were books, papers, and magazines. His head was bent, and he was busily scribbling in a notebook. Beneath the pull-down lamp his hair was the color of glazed clay pottery His back was a broad expanse of blue knit, and as she watched, he put his hand to the back of his neck and squeezed and massaged his neck muscles. Watching him while he was utterly unaware that he was not alone, he suddenly seemed to be truly human.

Iris emerged from the doorway. "What are you doing here, and where's Brenda?" She walked over to the table and grasped the knobs of a high-backed kitchen chair.

He closed the book with a snap and looked intently into her face. "How do you feel?"

"Where's Brenda?" she repeated.

"At play practice. I took her in. I told Miss Hanley I'd be back to pick her up at ten o'clock."

"You did wh-what? It wouldn't have hurt her to miss one practice." The floor was cold. Iris stood on one bare foot and rested the other on top of it.

He quirked a brow at her grumpiness. "There was no need for her to miss rehearsal. I was going in to get the prescription filled anyway. Do you feel better?"

"Yes," she said, and slumped down in the kitchen chair. She wasn't going to let him rile her. Nothing was worth risking the return of that headache.

"Why haven't you asked the doctor for something for those tension headaches? There's no need for you to suffer like that."

"I don't have them very often—only when something comes along that ties me in knots." Her direct gaze held his.

"I get the message. How about a cup of coffee?"

"Ill get it," she said testily.

"I'll get it." For a big man he moved fast. "Cream? Sugar?"

"Straight from the pot." She had to get him out of here. He was the cause of the headache, and she didn't want another. "Did you charge the prescription to me?"

"Of course not." He passed over the mugs, choosing instead the good cups and saucers. Then he brought the coffeepot to the table and poured some for her and himself. "It was just a couple of dollars. As long as I caused the headache, I can at least pay for getting it fixed." She looked up into blue eyes that flicked over her quickly.

Iris stared back, being careful to keep her features deceptively calm, masking her swirling thoughts. He sat down on the other side of the table and put the books and magazines he was using in a neat stack. A quick glance told Iris they were farming periodicals. It was on the tip of her tongue to say something sarcastic, but instead she stared hard at the rangy form lounging in her kitchen chair. It galled her to think of him being here in the house with her asleep upstairs.

He stared back. Iris felt her cheeks grow warm. She became suddenly and uncomfortably aware of the faded old sweatshirt she wore and the strings of hair that hung around her face. The lack of makeup didn't bother her, as she seldom used it. Unconsciously she smoothed the hair back from her forehead and hooked loose strands over her ears.

"You don't have to stay. I'll pick up Brenda."

"You need something to eat. How about a piece of toast?"

She looked at him as if he were warped. "Thanks, but no thanks. I can manage. I've been taking care of myself for a long time," she snapped.

"Thirty-two years, according to Brenda."

"Well . . . glory be!" Iris's laugh held a wealth of bitterness. "Lesson number one. Never leave the enemy alone with little sister. He's very clever at picking her brain."

"I'm not the enemy, Iris."

"If you're not, I hope never to have one." She raised the cup to her mouth and took a big gulp, almost scalding her tongue.

"Careful. You may get another headache."

He sipped his coffee slowly. She watched his hands. They dwarfed the thin cup but handled it easily. His fingers were long, his nails cut close, and he had a sprinkling of reddish-brown hair on the backs of his hands that trailed down to his knuckles. Strong, smooth hands, soft palms. How would they look after a day of shoveling corn, loading manure, moving hog houses, or fixing fence?

The clock on the shelf struck the quarter hour. The sound wafted into a small eternity of silence. Iris jumped up and carried her cup and saucer to the sink.

"You'll have to leave. I've got to get Brenda."

"I told you I was going to do it." He unfolded his long length out of the chair. "It takes fifteen minutes to get to the school, and kids are never out on time."

"How do you know? I don't want her waiting around in the dark outside an empty school."

"Miss Hanley said the practice would more than likely run until ten-fifteen. I've got plenty of time." His calm and easy take-over manner was wildly irritating to her. He came up behind her, reached around, and set his cup and saucer on the counter. He was so big he loomed over her, reminding her of the football player she'd dated in college who had a huge, perfectly proportioned body and an infinitesimal brain.

"As usual, you've covered all the bases." She moved sideways down the counter and picked up a towel to dry the cups, something she usually would not have bothered to do.

He leaned his slim hips against the counter and crossed his long legs at the ankles, drawing her attention to his Nikes and to her own ice-cold bare feet.

"You're beginning to annoy me, Iris," he stated coolly. "I've tried to take into consideration how hard it is for you to let go of a part of the farm operation, especially because you've handled things so well since your father died. From all accounts you're an even better farm manager than he was."

The statement about her father hurt; she tried to shrug it away. "You've had your share of the profits," she said defensively.

28

"I've no fault with that. But I want to participate in the management of the farm, and I've a perfect legal right to do so. Besides, if you and I can work together, there'll be no need to hire so much extra help. It'll cut expenses."

"Ahhh . . . now we're getting down to the nitty-gritty." She slapped the towel over the rack and turned on him. Her bare feet were planted far apart, and her clenched fists rested on her hips. Headache be damned! "How much help do you think you'll be around here? You don't know the first thing about attaching a loader to the tractor, or filling the silo, or catching and holding hogs so they can be castrated. Brenda will be more help at farrowing time than you'll be." At this point, driven by some unknown force, Iris was goaded into delivering one last taunt. "You can sit in that *cracker box* with your pencil and work on farm accounts. That's as much help as I expect out of you." The slightest flicker of anger appeared in John's eyes, then vanished with a return of his slightly annoyed expression.

"You know, Iris, you might be kind of pretty if you didn't scowl so much. You look as if you're constantly eating a sour pickle." Her mouth opened, closed. He tilted his head in a cocky manner. "I just can't help but wonder if there's a soft woman beneath all that bluster." He took a step, and his hands came down firmly on her shoulders, holding her still when she might have moved away from him. "Maybe I should find out," he said, as if to himself. "I've got one minute at least before I have to leave to pick up

Brenda." The gleam in his eye spoke of the pleasure he received from her surprise . . . and her sudden expression of vulnerability.

He caught her lips quickly, as though afraid she'd fight him. But astonishment had taken temporary advantage of her reason, and her brain refused to tell her muscles to move. The scent of his face and his breath pervaded her being; his mouth was firm, yet soft, his cheeks smooth, yet prickly with a shadow of the day's growth. His arms and shoulders seemed to swallow her, and she fought to stay above the tide of sensuousness his kiss was inspiring, but its force over-powered her, and she yielded, allowing her lips to become soft and to part. He lifted his head, and grinned down into smoky-blue eyes that flew open.

"It's true! There is a woman under there."

Weak from capitulation but strong in the face of his taunt, Iris stepped back and lifted her shoulders in a careless gesture. "Why not? I like sex as well as the next person." It was the only thing she could think of to say, and almost immediately she was ashamed of having said it—so much so that she didn't look back into his eyes, but concentrated on the alligator sewn on the breast of his shirt.

"I'll keep that in mind." He squeezed her arm. His mouth twitched, but he managed not to smile and kept his voice bland as he continued. "Next time we'll take it a step further."

"We'll do no damn such thing!" she hissed. *The toad! The wart!*

"No?" He tipped his head in skepticism. "Wouldn't you like to take step number two and see what happens?"

She gazed into his eyes, so astonishingly blue and luminous, and drew a quivering breath.

He was good-naturedly amused by her momentary speechlessness. "Time's up. I'll go for Brenda. You get some shoes on. I don't know if I can handle you with a headache *and* a cold."

After he left, Iris stood in the kitchen with her fists pressed to her temples. Several crude words slipped through her lips, a luxury she didn't allow herself unless she was alone and exasperated almost beyond endurance. She breathed deeply and tried to stem the tears of rage that were stinging her eyelids.

"You fool!" she muttered. She didn't know to whom she should direct her anger—John or herself. Maybe she could just blame the circumstances that brought him here.

She grasped the back of the kitchen chair. But to submit to his kiss that way. Worse, to respond. Sexual desire for John? Sheer lunacy! It was only a kiss, for heaven's sake, she chided herself. But it wasn't the kiss that bothered her; it was those feelings she'd had while she was kissing him back. For one short moment she'd been lost in the sweet, warm world of his embrace, and her body had responded like a love-starved spinster's. And the awful part was . . . he knew!

She moved down to the end of the table and looked

at the stack of books he'd been using. They were all farm-related. *Land Use*, *Grain Farming*, *Farmer's Weekly*, and several pamphlets from Iowa State University. She restacked them, wishing she had the nerve to toss them out the door.

Did the Navy ever recall retired officers? She asked herself the question while drawing a bath. He had to be an officer. She couldn't imagine that big frame poured into a pair of bell-bottomed pants. If there were a war, he'd be recalled, she mused, sinking down into the warm suds. Well, she couldn't pray for a war in order to get rid of him. The next best thing to hope for was that he'd have hay fever, or a bad back so he couldn't lift bales. Maybe the sight of a calf being born would make him sick. She lay back and fantasized about the harm that could befall a city man on the farm. Like tumbling into the septic tank! She chuckled, but only briefly.

Quickly then she got out of the tub, dried herself, and wiped the steam off the bathroom mirror. The face that looked back at her was scowling. The mouth was pressed tight and turned down at the corners. The brows above the squinted eyes were drawn almost together. Oh, for land's sake! She'd let that . . . that redheaded woodpecker do this to her! Cripes!

Standing nude before the bathroom mirror, Iris took the rubber band from the end of her braid and loosened her hair, all the while trying to relax her facial muscles. She tried parting her lips and lifting the corners. She raised her eyebrows as if questioning and brought her lower jaw out to stretch the skin beneath her chin. None of these seemed to help.

There is a soft woman under there. Why should his stupid words stick in her mind? Taking a deep breath, she puffed out her chest and grabbed the hairbrush. Starting straight back from her forehead she brushed with long, vigorous strokes. Iris was proud of her hair. She thought back to her high-school years, when she stood head and shoulders above any boy in her class, and how she had held onto the compliments she received because of her beautiful, thick, startling blond hair that proclaimed her Swedish ancestry. It had darkened very little since that time. She wore a big floppy hat in the summer to keep the sun from drying it out, and also to shade her face. Iris didn't work at getting a tan; it came naturally. Every morning during the months she worked outside she applied a layer of sun screen to her face and neck to protect her skin from the wind, the dust, and the sun's hot rays. She used very few cosmetics other than eye makeup and lipstick, and weeks went by when she didn't use either of those.

Forcibly restraining herself from spraying her body with her favorite fragrance, as a concession to her bruised ego, she slipped into her nightgown and her terrycloth robe and went back to her bedroom to find some slippers. She was going to have a talk with Brenda and find out just what she'd told *Mr. Woodpecker.*

Downstairs she turned off all the lights except the

33

one over the back door and the one over the kitchen sink. He wouldn't have the nerve to come in if the house was dark, or almost dark, she reasoned.

Iris sat in a kitchen chair and looked out the window toward the grove. The outside floodlights illuminated about a hundred feet of the yard all around the house. For eighty years there only had been trees and land to see out this window. In a few days there would be lights in the grove and a mobile home implanted there—complete with porch and a carport. Electric and telephone lines would hang over the drive for the first time. Oh, cripes! Had she really grown so old she couldn't bear to see things change? She should have sold out as soon as her father died. Old Mrs. Lang was alive then. She would have bought out her interest for Junior. If that had happened, Iris and Brenda would be well used to living in town by now, and she'd be used to teaching, putting up with the kids who took an art course simply because they thought it was an easy way to make a credit.

Headlights coming down the road brought her thoughts back from the "might have beens" and to the present. With interest rates so high, it was impossible to buy back John Lang's interest in the farm, so what to do now? The best you can, old girl, she told herself with just a twinge of self-pity. Stay here and suffer it out. Even if she did sell out to him now, there wasn't a teaching job to be had within a hundred miles, and to move Brenda away from her school and her horses would break her younger sister's heart.

The station wagon bounced up the long drive that curved behind the house and out to the road again in a wide U. The car pulled around and stopped opposite the back door. Iris sat where she was until she heard two doors slam and Brenda's excited voice talking a mile a minute.

"Come on in, John. It's T.G.I.F. night. No school tomorrow. There's an old Vincent Price movie on. Did you see *The Raven*? Yuk! He sends thrills down my spine. Tonight it's *The House of Usher.* I've only seen it twice."

"The house is dark. Your sister may be in bed." The deep masculine voice sounded slightly critical to Iris.

"Oh, no. That's a trick of hers so you won't come in."

The screen door slammed, and Iris fervently wished Brenda's head had been caught in it. Drat that kid! Would she ever pass out of this brainless stage?

"Oh, I see. Well, in that case I'll stay and watch the movie. The set in the motel room has terrible color, and I can only get one station."

"Super. Do you like popcorn?"

"Love it." They passed through the small narrow room she and Brenda called the mud room, and came into the kitchen. John took off his jacket and hung it on the back of the chair. "I'll even make the popcorn if you point me toward a heavy pan and let me have a little light."

Iris stood in the shadow and seethed. He had seen her. How could he not have seen her in that white terry

35

robe? Damn him again! Brenda flipped on the switch beside the door, and flooded the kitchen and the dining room with light.

"Oh, hi. John's going to stay and watch the movie with me." Brenda took the jar of popcorn out of the cabinet. "How's your head?"

"Better." Iris's eyes raked the big man, who was taking a bottle of oil from the shelf. "But it could get worse!"

"Take one of the capsules I brought from the drugstore," he said calmly. He took the heavy pan Brenda offered him, poured in the oil, and glanced at Iris. His face broke into a smile; friendly, as seen through Brenda's eyes, but smug, as seen through Iris's. "What do you know! Lady Godiva, as I live and breathe."

"Who's that?" Brenda jumped up onto the counter, banged her heels against the cabinet door, then pushed off first one sneaker and then the other, sending them flying across the room, the laces still neatly tied.

I've done something wrong. I know I have! Iris groaned silently as she watched her sister.

"Lady Godiva was the wife of an earl. She rode her horse naked through the streets of Coventry with only her long blond hair to cover her." John poured the corn into the pan and slapped on the lid.

"Why'd she do that?"

"To save the people from paying a tax."

"Who was naked, the horse or the woman?"

Iris grimaced. On leaden feet she went into the living room, sank down in a chair, and picked up a thick paperback novel. Lady Godiva be damned! She jerked open the drawer in the side table next to the chair, took out a rubber band, and secured her hair at the nape of her neck. She was too angry to sit still and read, so she stared at the pages, trying to tune out the pleasant chatter of the two in the kitchen.

Brenda flounced into the room, John trailing her. She flopped on the floor in front of the set, dug into her bowl of popcorn, and complained to Iris about not having turned on the television. John plunked a bowl down in Iris's lap, then sprawled out on the couch with his own, after taking off his shoes in the same way Brenda had done.

"What are you reading?" he asked without looking at her.

"Tiger's Woman."

"She reads historical romances," Brenda said between mouthfuls. "She won't let me read some of 'em."

"Who wrote it? Michener? Jakes?" His long legs reached halfway across the room.

"De Blasis."

"Never heard of him."

"It isn't a him, it's a her," Iris snapped. "There are jobs women can do every bit as well as men, and writing is one of them."

"Okay. I agree with that."

His sudden capitulation surprised her, and she bent her head to read the same paragraph for the fourth time. She wondered if he was here because he was

37

lonely. He was a handsome man, charming when he chose to be. There was an air of experienced masculinity about him that any husband-hungry woman would adore, Iris thought, betting that even at this moment Louise Hanley was sharpening her hunting tools. This community was a nice place to raise a family, but a lousy place to find an eligible man, and Iris thought wryly that she was going to have plenty of female company soon.

She turned pages in her book at regular intervals, looked up several times to find John's eyes on her, and was so unnerved she hadn't the slightest idea what she was reading or what was on the screen in front of her.

It was one of the most uncomfortable evenings of her life, and as it dragged on, Iris decided she hated Vincent Price for making the darn movie in the first place.

There was a loud thump on the back door, then another.

"What the hell was that?" John asked.

"Arthur. He runs and then jumps on the door when he wants our attention."

Brenda rolled over onto her back and kicked her heels on the floor, imitating a child having a temper tantrum. "Darn, darn, darn! I forgot to put Arthur in the barn . . . and this is the good part."

"I'll do it." John began to put on his shoes.

"Arthur is Brenda's responsibility," Iris snapped.

"As long as I'm leaving, I'll put him in the barn and she'll owe me a favor."

"Okay!" Brenda rolled back over onto her stomach. "I'll give you a friendship pin to wear on your shoe."

"You mean a safety pin with a bead on it? I wondered what that was all about."

"Some kids have fifty pins, all from different friends."

"Yours might be the only one I ever get," he said, glancing down at Iris.

"Don't forget your books." She got up to follow him back through the dining room.

"You didn't eat your popcorn."

"I'll give it to Arthur in the morning."

"You should eat something before you go to bed." He put on his jacket.

" 'Bye, John. See ya tomorrow," Brenda called.

"Thanks for taking her and bringing her home." Iris said the words begrudgingly.

"Sure. Good night."

Iris, waiting beside the door to switch off the lights, heard John swear. His curse was swiftly followed by a booming "I-r-is! What the hell has this dog been into?"

She looked out the window, and there was Arthur frolicking around John, smeared from one end to the other with . . . A slow smile started in her eyes as realization dawned, and spread to her lips. She had to use every bit of her willpower to keep from laughing.

She opened the door a crack. "What do you mean?" she asked innocently.

"What's this stuff all over him?" John was moving back and forth, trying to keep away from Arthur, who was sure John had come out to play with him.

"Oh, that? That's fresh cow manure. He rolls in it several times each spring. I've never figured out the attraction. Just take hold of his collar and he'll go along with you to the barn. Brenda will give him a bath tomorrow."

"There's no place on his collar where I can . . . He's covered with the stuff! Phew!"

"Sure, there is. Just take him to the barn, and tomorrow you'll get a friendship safety pin to go on your shoe."

Iris shut the door and leaned back against it, with her hand over her mouth to stifle the giggles. When she peeked out the window again John had the dog by the collar. He was almost bent double in an effort to keep Arthur from rubbing against his long legs, while half leading, half dragging him to the barn. She laughed until tears blurred her vision and she had to mop them away with the front of her robe so she could see him standing beneath the yard light wiping his hands on a handkerchief.

The movie had ended when she returned to the living room. She flicked off the set, still giggling, and couldn't seem to stop.

"Why did you do that?" Brenda sat up, cross-legged. "And what's the matter with you?"

"Which question do you want answered first?"

"I don't care."

40

"The movie was over, and you're not particularly interested in the news." Iris couldn't stop grinning. "What's so funny about that?"

"It's Arthur and the . . . woodpecker." Iris went into a fit of laughter. Brenda sat with her mouth twisted to one side, waiting. "He was . . ." Another spasm of laughter. "It was so funny. Serves him right, too."

"What happened?"

Iris wiped her eyes on the robe. "Arthur has rolled in fresh manure again." Giggles followed every word. "You'll have to give him a bath in the morning."

"Oh, no! That lousy dog! That worthless hunk of hair and bone!"

"You know how it gets caked up around his . . . neck?" More giggles interrupted her. "John couldn't find a place to hold onto him so he could get him to . . . the . . . barn." Iris clasped her hands over her stomach. "*Justice*. Justice comes to those who wait," she said smugly, still smiling.

"Poor John. I think you're mean to laugh."

"Poor John, my foot! He needs our sympathy like a hole in the head."

"I think he's cute. Or he would be if he wasn't so . . . so *old!* Miss Hanley's beady eyes lit up like a Christmas tree when she saw him. 'Certainly, Mr. Lang. Yes, Mr. Lang. I wouldn't dream of letting Brenda leave the building until I'm sure you're here, Mr. Lang.' Bossy old toad! She couldn't wait to find out all about him." Brenda gave her sister a sly smile. "I filled the old biddy's ear full. I said he was going to be living here at the farm with us and that you and John were almost—"

"Almost what?" Iris sank onto a chair.

"That you were good friends and almost in love."

"Brenda Ouverson! I could shake you. Why in the world did you say such a thing? It'll be all over the school tomorrow."

"So what? At least I put the kibosh to her plans."

"Oh, mercy! Nothing but marriage puts the kibosh to Louise's plans when she goes after a man. What did you tell *him* about me besides how old I am?"

"Not much. We went to the Hamburger Hut before he took me to school. He asked about your headaches and a few things like that."

"After this keep your lip buttoned. Don't discuss me with him, Brenda. The whole situation is difficult enough without your giving him extra ammunition to use against me."

Later Iris lay in bed and listened to her sister move about in her room. Had she been too hard on her? Brenda passed the door on her way to the bathroom. "Iris," came the wail in a few moments.

"What's the matter?" Iris asked, pushing herself up on an elbow.

"I dropped my toothbrush in the toilet."

Iris sank back down on the bed. "Your problem," she called.

"But . . . my teeth will be all hairy by morning!"

"It's either that or fish it out and use it."

"Yuk!"

42

Iris listened to Brenda's grumblings. She was responsible for shaping that young life, and at times she questioned how good a job she was doing. Suddenly her mind was crowded with memories of lips warm and gentle, of arms strong and unrelenting. The next time we'll take it a step further, he'd said. She flopped over on her stomach and buried her face in the pillow, but she couldn't block the image of smiling eyes and dull red hair from her mind.

Three

Wednesday.

The mobile home arrived, and changed the look of the homestead forever. Iris watched through the kitchen window, tears rolling down her cheeks.

Begrudgingly, she admitted that John had been careful to see that the least possible damage was done to the yard when the truck pulling the seventy-foot house backed it into the grove. Boards were placed so the huge wheels didn't make deep ruts in the sod, and the men were careful not to scrape the bark from the trees, whose lower branches had been trimmed when the utility pole was set.

Iris turned from the window and wiped her eyes and her nose on the tissue she had balled in her hand. Life as she had known it here on the homestead of her ancestors was over. What she hated about the house, she told herself, was that it was so damned *new!* She had tried to banish thoughts of its owner from her

43

mind, but his image turned up at the oddest times—when she was feeding the horses, drawing water for the sows, washing the dishes. She was disgusted with herself for responding to his kiss like a love-starved spinster; the memory made her feel sick and empty.

During the next week, Iris worked harder than she had ever worked in her life, while doing her best to ignore the activity going on in *her* grove. While she was moving A-frame hog houses out in last year's alfalfa field with the tractor and loader and preparing them to house the pregnant sows, workers were building a foundation under the cracker box, as she thought of it, adding a long screened porch, and attaching a carport with redwood slabs on the side facing the county road. Coarse gravel was hauled in to make a drive, and a new mailbox went up alongside hers.

Every day Brenda leaped from the school bus to see what progress had been made. She was thrilled with the idea of a neighbor in the grove, and completely enthralled with John D. Lang, Jr. Iris tried hard to make allowances for her sister's youthful enthusiasm and not feel deserted.

"You should see it, Iris. It's got a ceiling fan, a microwave oven, and . . . everything."

The days were getting longer as spring approached, and it was still light when they ate dinner now. Iris no longer sat at the end of the table, where she could look out at the grove.

"That's nice," she said absently. "Do you have play

44

practice? If you do, let's get the dishes done. I have things to do while you're gone."

"Yeah, darn it. John was going to build a fire in his fireplace tonight."

"I think you and I should have a little talk right now." Iris's voice held a no-nonsense tone.

"What about?" Brenda said tiredly. "What have I done wrong now?"

"Nothing. You haven't done anything wrong. I've never had to worry about your doing . . . anything *wrong,* after I've explained things to you. You're a very sensible girl for your age."

"Okay. You've built me up. What don't you want me to do?" Brenda looked bored with the conversation, but her fingers were nervously pulling a slice of bread into small pieces.

"Honey, I don't want you spending so much time over there." Iris jerked her head toward the grove. "He's a single man living alone and you're a fourteen-year-old girl."

"Well, so what? I like him, even if you don't!"

"It isn't a matter of liking him or not liking him, Brenda. I don't want you spending a lot of time there. People . . . will talk."

"What about?"

"Well, they don't know him, and they might think—"

"You mean they'll think I'm sleeping with him?"

"Oh, heavens!" Iris looked at the ceiling and then back at her sister's sullen face. "Yes, they might. You know how narrow-minded some people are."

"Yeah." Brenda's face was still rebellious. "It would be just like Stanley's mother to spread around something like that, but it'd be about you, not me."

"I don't want her spreading anything about either of us."

"Can I tell John I won't be over to see him break in the fireplace?"

"When he sees us leave he'll remember about play practice."

It was almost dark when Iris backed the pickup out of the garage. Lights shone from the house in the grove. It was painted a dark green now, although the pressed wood siding had come from the factory a light tan. Iris reluctantly admitted it didn't look as out of place as she'd thought it would, but still she didn't like having it there.

After parking the pickup beside several others, Iris went into the school with Brenda. They walked down the silent hall to the gym-cum-auditorium, which had a stage across one end and pull-down metal bleachers on the sides. The drama teacher sat at a desk near the door.

"Hello, Iris. Are you going to watch dress rehearsal? Brenda's doing splendidly."

"I don't think so, Louise. I have a few errands to do. What time will you finish?"

"About nine. We'll have one more short practice on Wednesday. Brenda said Mr. Lang is planning to come to the play."

"Is that right? I hadn't heard anything about it."

Iris tried to wipe the annoyance off her face.

"She seemed quite sure. Also, I've been intending to visit and ask you to help me choose colors for a needlework wall hanging I want to start."

I just bet you have, Iris thought, but aloud she said, "Do that, Louise. I'll be glad to help you."

At the supermarket Iris dug a list out of her pocket and went up and down the aisles filling her grocery cart. She shopped carefully, resisting impulse buying, which ballooned her budget out of control. When she finished she eased her cart up to the check-out counter.

"Hello, Iris. How ya doin'?"

"Fine, Linda. You?"

"Fine. I hear your partner's moved a mobile home out to the farm. I haven't seen him yet, but I hear he's quite a guy. Having a man around should take a load off you, huh, Iris?"

Iris smiled and agreed for appearance's sake. Then she greeted Denny, the boy bagging the groceries.

He grinned shyly. "Is Brenda at play practice?"

"Dress rehearsal. I've got to pick her up as soon as I get the groceries home."

Pushing her cart, the boy followed Iris to the truck. She opened the door of the cab and stepped aside. "I'd like to stop by sometime and see Brenda's horse. That is, if it's okay with you."

"Of course, Denny. But you'd better check with Brenda to be sure she's home."

"I'll do that. Thanks."

As Iris waited at the stoplight on the highway, her thoughts were disconnected. A boy wanted to visit Brenda . . . everyone was talking about John Lang . . . some of the sows had to be rebred and some sold because they were past three years old . . .

The light turned green, and she followed the two-lane highway to the blacktop and turned north, and a mile later, west on the gravel. She knew every foot of the road; she had driven it a thousand times.

It was strange to come down the road and see lights twinkling in the grove. Iris turned into the drive and glanced at the sleek station wagon parked in the carport. I wonder how long he'll last out here in the boonies, she mused. He's seen most of the exotic places in the world—he won't be content to stay here. When he goes I hope he takes that . . . trailer with him. Her thoughts were still running rampant as she picked up an armload of groceries.

"Let me help you." The voice came suddenly, from behind her.

"Oh, good heavens! You scared me to death!" All the color drained from her face, and her smoky eyes were suddenly large.

"I'm sorry." John took the bag out of her arms. "I didn't mean to frighten you. I thought you saw me coming across the drive."

"I'm not used to having people sneak up on me," she said crossly, her heart thumping up a storm.

"Hand me the other sack. I can take both of them."

Iris put it in his arm and picked up a smaller one.

She walked ahead of him into the house and flipped on the light switch. John set the sacks beside hers on the kitchen counter. The close contact with his tall frame made Iris step back quickly.

"You *are* jumpy, aren't you? You've been working too hard. You don't have to work yourself to death in order to avoid me, you know." He began taking the groceries from the sacks and putting them on the counter.

"I'd have to be out of my mind if I didn't try to avoid a headache, wouldn't I?"

"Am I still such a thorn in your side?" he asked, on his way to the refrigerator with a carton of milk.

"More like a pain in the ass," she said bluntly, without thinking.

He laughed as he moved to reach over her shoulder and pick up another carton of milk. "That's what I like about you. I don't have to wonder for a minute what you're thinking."

Iris skirted him to get to the freezer to put away the frozen mini-pizzas that were Brenda's favorite snack. She watched him warily as he crossed the room, stopping at the window to look out toward the grove. Palms out, his hands slid into the back pockets of his faded jeans. His forearms were bare, the cuffs of his shirt casually rolled to just below his elbows. Iris noticed how the muscles of his shoulders and back stirred the cloth of his denim shirt. If his size hadn't been enough to distinguish him, certainly his bearing and that head of dark red hair would have been.

"I see you've pulled the curtains," he said, fingering the thin white cotton panels that had formerly been tied back.

"I usually do in the summer."

"Liar. It isn't summer yet." He turned and leveled his gaze on her.

"That's what I like about *you*. I don't have to wonder what *you're* thinking." She turned his words on him.

"I'm glad there's something about me you like." He raked her with his gaze; starting at the top of her head, he took in every feature of her face, her throat, her breasts. His eyes lingered there for a long moment before moving back up to her face again. "You have magnificent hair. I like it done up like that on the top of your head. You look very stately, very controlled."

"Oh, sure!" She shifted, uncomfortable under his intent perusal. "You'll have to excuse me. I've got to pick up Brenda."

Iris went out onto the narrow enclosed back porch, where the chore clothes were hung and smelly barn-yard boots were left on a rubber mat. She waited for him to pass so she could turn out the light and lock the door. He walked purposefully toward her, then stopped.

"You're a fraud, Iris Ouverson," he whispered, and brazenly winked at her. "You're not as crusty as you pretend to be." Ten seconds dragged by while Iris drew a shallow breath, followed by a deeper one. She could see his eyes were full of laughter. "I may have to kiss you again."

She cleared her throat and swallowed hard, then said bravely, "Stop horsing around and get out of here. I don't want—"

"Brenda waiting around outside an empty school." He finished the sentence for her. His hands slid along her upper arms. Slowly he drew her closer to him, until she was pressed against his long length. He lowered his head and nuzzled the hair above her ear. His fingers found their way under her jacket to stroke her back. "I'm glad you're tall. I don't have to bend so far to kiss you." He settled his lips against her mouth and breathed. "I like the way you taste, too. Like a nice, cool, vanilla ice cream cone."

Iris came to her senses and struggled against him, but he refused to loosen his hold. His strength won out, and she ceased her efforts to escape. Soon she was incapable of moving, of protesting. The warmth of his body held her like a magnet, and it was easy to lean against his large masculine frame and surrender to the delicious floating feeling.

The lips that touched hers were warm and sweet as they tingled across her mouth with fleeting, feathery kisses. The arms holding her gradually tightened. His feet moved apart, making his stance wider, and she felt herself being drawn against, then between, hard, muscular thighs that held hers. A longing to love and be loved washed over her. The kiss became more possessive, deepened, her lips parted, his tongue touched hers, and his hand slid over her breast.

She wondered if he could feel the pounding of her heart beneath his hand. His hand? On her breast? Oh! For crissake! She didn't behave this way! She stiffened. He sensed it immediately and loosened his hold, but he didn't release her.

Iris was breathless when he pulled his mouth from hers and raised his head only a fraction to look down into her face.

"Your eyes are the color of the sea around Palau Island in the Pacific." His whisper was deep and husky. "They change like the sea, too. Sometimes calm, sometimes stormy. I've yet to see them happy and sparkling." He placed a gentle kiss on her forehead. "Try not to resent me so much." His breath was ragged as he gently moved her away from him. "Come on. Let's go get little sister."

The past few minutes had robbed Iris of all logical thought. She stood stupefied for several seconds before she realized he was waiting for her to go out the door. He followed close behind her, turned out the light, and tested the doorknob to make sure it was locked before he shut the door.

Iris automatically went to the driver's side of the pickup but was gently nudged out from under the wheel by John's solid bulk. "I'll drive," he said quietly, and she mindlessly moved over. He fumbled for the lever so he could move the seat back to accommodate his long legs, then started the truck and turned on the headlights. She knew he was looking at her, but she stared stoically out the window, and was relieved when he put the truck in motion.

Iris was thankful for the darkness. Her face burned with embarrassment. She was so disgusted with herself she could have screamed. She was mad! She was a fool! What had possessed her to participate in that . . . little display? She stifled a groan as her mind began summoning back, in feverish detail, the feel of his lips, his arms, and how she had melted into them. Even now the scent of peppery male cologne assaulting her nostrils was doing crazy things to her hormones.

The truck left the gravel road and pulled out onto the blacktopped highway, headed toward the school. The silence was heavy. Not a word had passed between them since they'd left the farm. What the heck do I care what he thinks? she wondered bitterly. I don't even like him!

"Who is Stanley?" His words boomed into the silence.

"What did you say?" She knew, but she had to get her head together.

"Who is Stanley?" he repeated in a quieter tone.

"He's a fellow who lives up the road. We just passed his place. He helps out sometimes when I get in a crunch."

"Do you pay him?"

She met his glance with a pretense of calm. "Sometimes. Other times we trade work. It's a tradition around here to pitch in and help a neighbor if you can."

"What do you do for him?"

"I may spend half a day plowing, spraying, or culti-vating for him." His questions were beginning to irri-tate her.

"I can relieve you of that. Do you date him?"

"Who? Stanley?" She hesitated, then said, "Some-times." He needn't know that she despised Stanley, who had a hint of a pot belly, though a very well-developed dirty mind.

"The football coach at the high school has been coming out to see you, too, hasn't he?"

"Will you kindly stop pumping my sister?"

He laughed. "You don't have to pump Brenda. Once her mouth gets in gear there's no stopping it. She said the coach had just recently separated from his wife."

There was nothing Iris could add to that. A car swept down the road toward them, the headlights flashing over John's face. His bottom lip was drawn between his teeth, and his brows were beetled into a frown.

There was another long, tense silence. Iris stared at the ribbon of highway and was thankful when the school came into view. John slowed the truck and turned into the parking lot. There were more cars and trucks there than when Iris had brought Brenda, so she knew the rehearsal wasn't over yet. John realized that, too. He turned off the headlights and turned in the seat to look at her. Damn! Why had he parked directly beneath a streetlight?

"Am I going to have to make an appointment with you to discuss my work schedule?"

"Work schedule? There's no schedule on a farm. You do what has to be done no matter how long it takes. If there's any schedule it's from daylight till dark." She hunched down in the seat and looked away from him.

After a brief silence he said flatly, "Are you going to tell me what I can do to help you, or are you going to leave me to skid my wheels?"

"What can you do, for heaven's sake? I spelled it out on the report. This year we're putting in corn, beans, and alfalfa. We have forty sows that produce almost three hundred and fifty pigs a year, and after planting we'll get about fifty feeder calves. You can sure as hell clean out the hog houses, if you want, and—"

"Why do you use the A-frames? Why not put all your sows in the farrowing building?"

The question angered her. "Farrowing building? We don't have such a thing. What we have is a converted chicken house. I put the older sows there and the younger ones out in the A-frames. If I'm careful I farrow them five times a year and have hogs ready for market every couple of months. It's quick money even if the market isn't what it should be."

"I've seen what you use for a farrowing building. Could we add on to it?"

"We could do a lot of things if we had the money," she snapped.

"Would you like me to take charge of the hog operation?"

This question stunned her. "Mercy! What does a

sailor know about hogs, except that they make bacon and ham?"

"You'd be surprised." He grinned wickedly. "And here's another little bit of information for you to file away and chew on later. I can attach a loader to a tractor, and what's more, I can fix the engine if something goes wrong."

"You're kidding! Well, glory be! A mechanically inclined sailor!" She made it sound like something that just crawled out from under a rock. John's grin faded.

"Knock off the sarcasm, Iris. You may find out that I know a little something beyond coiling rope and climbing rigging."

"I didn't think they did that anymore," she said lamely. "And I'm sorry. I was surprised, that's all."

"It's okay. I didn't expect you to jump with joy. What's on the bill for tomorrow?"

"A stock buyer will be here in the morning to pick up our marketable hogs. We have about sixty that weigh between two hundred twenty and two hundred forty pounds. After that we spread manure on the forty acres to the south and commercial fertilizer on the rest of the plowed ground. I don't believe in 'land bank.' I use every foot of our four hundred acres."

"I gathered that from your annual report. You don't use many insecticides and herbicides, either. I agree with that." A large hand reached out, and firm fingers turned her face toward him. "It's been a long, hard row for you to hoe, working the farm alone. I don't want to take anything away from you. I want to help you, if you'll let me. I'm as green as spring grass when it comes to farming. All I know is what I've read in books. I'd appreciate it if you'd be patient and teach me. In return I'll bring my mechanical skill and I guarantee you our farm machinery will be kept in tip-top condition."

"That'll be a help. The tractor men charge an arm and a leg every time they come out to fix something." She felt breathless, and foolish, and . . . small. She moved her chin out of his hand when she heard a car door slam. "I haven't been very nice, have I? I'm not usually so bitchy."

"You've been carrying quite a load. Are there other lady farmers around here?"

"A couple of widows who hire people to do the work. Kids are coming out now, John. Brenda will see the truck."

Several cars peeled out of the school parking lot, and Iris gritted her teeth to think that Brenda was reaching the age of the kids driving those cars. Brenda ran to the truck and flung open the door.

"Can we give Jerry a ride home? Purple pot roast!" she blurted when she saw that Iris wasn't alone. "Hi, John. Why didn't ya come in? You'd've made ol' lady Hanley's day!"

"We can give you a ride home, Jerry," Iris said to the boy standing behind her sister.

"Thanks. I'll ride back here." He dropped a canvas bag in the truck bed.

"Sit up here, Jerry. It's too cold back there," Brenda protested, and nudged Iris over toward John. "We sit four lots of times, don't we, Iris?"

Iris didn't answer. John shifted his weight, and she moved close to him. Her hip was tight against his, her thigh lay along his, and her shoulder was tucked behind him.

"A little more; Jerry can't close the door." Brenda turned, and Iris pressed closer to John. The door slammed.

"Are we all in?" John asked, and Iris heard him mutter, "Humm . . . nice."

"Brenda could sit on my lap," Jerry said after a small hesitation.

"I'd smash your legs. This is much better. Now, if only ol' lady Hanley'd come out and see Iris sitting close to John, it'd pay her back for being a grouch."

Iris sucked in a breath, and John laughed. "Oh, to be so young and so uninhibited. Were you like that when you were her age, Iris?" He turned his eyes from the road, and for a few seconds she felt his breath on her face.

"I was so shy that I hardly opened my mouth for fear someone would look at me. I've always encouraged Brenda to speak out, though, to realize that she is entitled to express an opinion. Now I think I might have done better to have taught her a little tact, too."

John's soft chuckle made his rib cage vibrate against her. "Tell me which way to go, Jerry."

Iris's shoulder was pressed firmly behind John's, her

58

chin practically resting on his shoulder. She had only to move her eyes to see his profile. He was smiling. She wondered if it was because he could feel her heart pounding through the breast that was crushed against him.

"It's right on your way—that is, if you're going home, sir."

"You can call him John. He won't mind," Brenda said smugly. "He lives with us out—"

"Brenda," Iris interrupted quickly. She couldn't sit by and witness the demolition of her reputation. "Let me explain, please. The three of us own the farm jointly, Jerry. The purchase was made for John while he was serving in the Navy. Now that he's out of the service he's going to live on the farm for a while in a tenant house. He does *not* live with us."

"I know all that, Miss Ouverson. I knew how it was. I live at the next place, Mr. Lang. Just pull up there by the mailbox and let me out. Thanks a lot for the ride. I'll be sure and set everyone straight 'bout that, Miss Ouverson. 'Bye, Brenda."

When the door closed, Iris shifted to the middle of the seat and groaned. No one had to set anyone straight about anything, dammit. There was nothing to set straight!

"Do you really let it bother you that people might talk about my living out at the farm?" John asked as soon as they were on the road again.

"This is small town, USA. Of course I don't want to be gossiped about."

"Maybe we should get married," he teased, a broad smile splitting his face.

"Yeah!" Brenda let out a whoop.

"Shut up, you two, and be serious!"

"We'll leave lights on in both houses all night long to throw the gossip spies off the trail," John said. He lowered his voice to a sinister whisper. "And if I come over I'll wait until after dark and wear a black raincoat and slouch hat. Then I'll case the joint before I ring the doorbell."

"We can put one of those bell things across the drive that rings when a car goes over it," Brenda said between giggles. "If it rings while you're in our house you can hide in the basement."

"I could wear a skirt and a shawl and be your old-maid aunt." His laugh rang out, joined by Brenda's, and Iris couldn't hold hers back any longer.

"A six-foot-four Amazon aunt?"

"I'll walk on my knees. See how far I'm willing to go to preserve your reputation?"

By the time they reached the farm they were all laughing together as if they were playing some gigantic joke on the entire county. John let the sisters out and pulled the pickup into the garage. Brenda went into the house, and Iris waited beside the back door. John came toward her swinging the car keys on his finger.

"Come on over and take a look at the *tenant* house," he said, smiling down at her. "We can begin the secret maneuvers tomorrow."

"I was hoping you'd ask us." Brenda squeezed out the back door, almost knocking Iris off the step. "Wait till I put Arthur in the barn. I don't want him rolling in any more cow pies!"

Iris glanced up at the tall man watching her. The yard light was bright enough so she could see the sparkle in his eyes. His face was creased with a smile, and he was breathtakingly handsome. Her eyes couldn't seem to leave his face, and she was unaware that she, too, was smiling.

"Finally." He bent closer, and she could feel his warm breath. "Finally, I see the happy sea. Gentle waves shining in the sun." Her lips parted, but no words came. "Speechless? Good. I like you that way once in a while, too."

Four

Iris stood just inside the door, not believing that she was really here in the hated house with the *woodpecker,* and that she'd come willingly. She shoved her hands down into the pockets of her jacket, hunched her shoulders, and looked around. The small entry was tiled and surrounded by plush sculptured carpet. She and Brenda slipped out of their boots, a habit acquired by people who work with the soil.

John moved about the living room turning on lights. It was a step lower than the rest of the house, with a prefabricated fireplace on one side and a large picture window on the other. There was a leather couch and

61

chair with a large matching ottoman, end tables and lamps, bookcases, and a television/stereo combination beneath the window.

"Very nice," Iris murmured. "It's larger than it looks from the outside."

"Come see the rest." John led the way into the dining-kitchen area, which was divided from the living room by an ornamental iron railing.

"I've seen it, so I'll turn on the TV." Brenda suited action to words and plunked down on the floor not three feet from the screen. It was on the tip of Iris's tongue to tell her to move back, but she doubted her sister would even hear because the volume was so loud.

The kitchen was well planned, with floor-to-ceiling cabinets, spacious wood-topped counters, and the latest model appliances, including a microwave oven. Iris smiled her approval and followed John down the narrow hallway. He stopped at the first doorway.

"I've put my desk and a lot of my books in this room." He switched on the light and stepped aside so she could see. Her shoulder brushed his chest as she angled her body to squeeze through the doorway, which he practically blocked.

One large hand came out and cupped the back of her head and gently stroked her hair upward toward the swirl on the top. She moved quickly away from him, trying to quell the stirrings in her love-starved body.

"Very nice," she murmured, although at the moment she wasn't seeing anything.

"The bathroom has a garden tub as well as a shower stall," John explained when they reached it. "I'll never use the tub, but I wouldn't have known what to do with the space if they'd taken it out."

The tub was gigantic, set in a corner, and enclosed by peach curtains. Iris couldn't suppress a small laugh.

"Awful, isn't it?" John's eyes twinkled as he watched her. "You have to take the bad with the good. I did get the lavatory cabinet built high enough so I won't break my back every time I wash my face."

"I've often wondered if the people who put in bath fixtures think everyone who uses them is four foot one." She stared into warm blue eyes and suddenly felt much smaller than her five ten.

"We wouldn't have to worry about that, would we?" He was grinning now. Iris moved back. He was too close!

"About what?" She could smell the freshness of his breath. Irrational anxiety bubbled up inside her.

"About having four-foot-one offspring."

Iris didn't realize she was holding her breath, until the air came rushing out in one long puff. "Humph!" was all she could say. His shoulders, the broad chest, smiling face framed with dark red hair not only filled her eyes, but her thoughts, her mind, the center of her self.

She tried for lightness in her voice. "Is this all I get on the fifty-cent tour?"

"You have to pay the guide now." His voice lowered

to a raspy tone. "I'm going to kiss you, Iris Ouverson. What'er'ya gonna do about it?"

Iris felt the blood rush around her body. She looked at him through thick, curled lashes and knew she wasn't going to do anything. She wanted him to hold her, kiss her, make a thousand little memories for her to tuck away and bring out in the dark of the night when she lay in her lonely bed. She turned her eyes away. He was too astute at reading her thoughts.

John reached out and cupped the nape of her neck with long, warm fingers and pulled her toward him. The smile had left his face, and his eyes held an indescribable expression. Was it tenderness? Iris felt her strength drain out through her toes, leaving her swaying against his tower of strength.

"Ah . . . huh . . . Brenda . . ." she said feebly.

"God bless CBS or NBC or whatever."

"But . . . I don't want you to kiss me."

"Sure, you do."

"Nooo . . ." She shook her head, and her lips moved across his.

"Do that again. I like it." The arm about her waist held her snugly against him, and his hand moved caressingly over the softness of her bottom, then pried into the hip pocket of her jeans. "I've kissed you three times. Each time I liked it better than the time before."

"Two times," she whispered.

"Three. One time you were asleep. Now, hush, and let me get on with it."

"You . . . had no right . . ."

"Your lips are pressed together again. You're being stubborn." He clicked his tongue censoriously. "I'll have to kiss you until they soften. If we're in here much longer, Brenda will come in."

"You're a toad!"

"Turn me into a prince." He kissed her with slow deliberateness, his lips playing, coaxing. Her breath caught painfully in her throat, and then, with a deep sigh, she parted her lips against his and slowly traced the curve of his bottom lip with the warm, moist stroking of her tongue. He opened his mouth and caught the tip gently between his teeth. A flood of pleasure washed over her, sending excitement coursing through her veins. It was strange, because she'd never before wanted to kiss anyone like this.

He raised his head after several hard, quick kisses. His eyes, half closed, looked down his nose into her eyes. His hands were everywhere; on her back, the sides of her breasts, on her rounded bottom. "Have you noticed how well we fit together?" The words came on the fragment of a breath.

"No!" The hands on his chest began to push. She wanted to jerk away, but she was held fast. Make it light, she told herself, treat this situation as if it's no big deal.

He had hold of her hand now and was leading her past a washer and dryer set in an alcove with sliding doors to hide them from view.

The bedroom was the width of the house. A closet with mirrored doors ran along one side; a queen-sized bed with a headboard for books and a reading light occupied the opposite wall. The end of the room was solid, with small windows. Six stacks of drawers were built in beneath them, covered with a wide ledge. Several framed pictures, a shell inlaid box, and a small bronze statue resided there.

"What in the world will you put in so many drawers?" Iris thought it a reasonable question, considering . . .

John laughed and squeezed her hand. "I never had enough space aboard ship. Maybe I did go a little wild. They're only half full." He turned her toward the full-length mirror on the closet doors, put his hands on her shoulders, and pulled her back against him. She stared at the smiling face above her right shoulder. He lowered his head and pressed his cheek to hers. "Don't you think we make a handsome couple?"

She looked at her slenderness in the jeans and shirt. Her waist was small, her breasts soft and rounded, but her makeup free face—blaa! She was so ordinary! What was there about her that could possibly attract a man like John D. Lang, Jr.?

"We've got to go. School tomorrow, and the hog buyer will be here bright and early." It wasn't hard to put a chill in her voice when she spoke. She pulled away from him and walked quickly back to the living room. "Let's go, Brenda."

"Ohhhh . . . This is about over. Just ten more minutes, Iris. Pl-eee-ze!"

"Well, turn it down. Heavens! You'll be deaf by the

time you're twenty." She stood beside her boots and the jacket that lay on the floor next to them.

"Are you going to stand up for ten minutes, or sit down and have a cup of coffee?" John leaned casually against the refrigerator. "It's leftover, but I can warm it up in the microwave."

"Well, all right. Ten minutes, and then Brenda's got to go home and get to bed." She sat down at the table and tried not to stare at him as he poured coffee into two mugs. She had to be out of her mind. Worse than Louise Hanley. A cold shiver raced through her body. She couldn't let him get to her! She didn't want to like him too much! He would go . . . and then what?

John sat down across from her. "How long have you been taking care of your sister?"

"Almost all her life. She was born during my first year at college. Her mother left before she was a year old, and Dad had a woman come out from town to care for her. I finished college in three years and came home to look after both of them. My plans were to find a teaching job when Brenda started school. I did, but driving forty miles every morning in Iowa winter weather got pretty tough." Why was she rattling on like this?

"Does Brenda's mother come to see her?"

"She came once, just before Daddy died. It was the longest week of my life. Daddy was given custody of Brenda when he and her mother divorced. When he died, custody was transfered to me. I'm her guardian until she reaches legal age."

"Is it possible Brenda's mother might want her one day?"

"She can't have her!" Iris said heatedly, and felt a flush rise in her cheeks. The beast! Why did he have to bring up her old fear? "I've taken care of Brenda practically all her life. I'm all she has; she's all I have. I've done my best to teach her to be a decent human being, to respect herself and others. When she's able to take care of herself, I'll cut her loose from my apron strings, but not until!" Her lips quivered when she finished, and a bleakness came into her eyes. She'd recently begun to wonder what in the world she would do when Brenda grew up and left her.

"Bringing up a child alone isn't easy, is it?" John's hand reached across and covered hers.

"You two got to the hand-holding stage already? Wow!" Brenda bounded up the step to the kitchen like a lively colt.

"Don't sit down," Iris cautioned. "We're going."

"Oh, shoot! Dumb old school. Just six more weeks and it'll all be over."

Iris tried to pull her hand free, but John's fingers curled around her wrist, and he turned her hand palm up. He rubbed his thumb across the long, slender fingers, with their neatly clipped, unpolished nails, while his eyes held hers captive.

"It's hard to believe these hands have done all this work."

"Believe it, buster! Farming is more than planting in the spring, harvesting in the fall, and watching the sky

68

in between. Yours won't be so soft six weeks from now." Iris gave her hand a yank, almost upsetting her coffee. She got up quickly, jerking on her jacket and shoving her feet into her boots. She didn't know why his remark about her hand had made her so angry. "Thanks for the tour and the coffee. C'mon, Brenda." She looked up to see her sister standing with her palms raised, her shoulders hunched, and a quizzical look on her face, while she stared up at John.

"Brenda!" The order shot out sharply as hurt pierced her heart. The action represented a conspiracy between them . . . against her. For the first time in her life she felt her sister's loyalty slipping away from her.

"Iris! Guess what? We've got baby rabbits!" Brenda stood in the mud room stripping off her chore clothes.

Iris glanced at the clock; it was just six-thirty in the morning. "You've finished your chores already?"

"Sure have. John helped me. He took care of the lambs and the hogs. I'm glad. Phew, they stink."

"The lambs are your project, Brenda. You wanted them. Besides, he doesn't know anything about what we've been feeding our animals."

"I told him how much oats and lamb finisher. He wrote it down on a card and put it in his pocket. The same with the cows, horses, and those darned old smelly pigs. I fed the rabbits." Brenda went to the sink and washed her hands. "Elizabeth had eight babies. Boy, are they cute. John said maybe we could get a goat."

69

"A goat? What the heck for?" Iris dumped a can of tomatoes into the crock pot.

"For fun. He said the sheep could be in the orchard if he put up an electric fence. Would you care if we got a donkey?" Brenda sat down at the table and began to butter toast.

While the electric can opener worked on the top of another can of tomatoes, Iris took a plate of bacon and eggs out of the warming oven and set them on the table in front of her sister. "You and John were so busy talking I'm surprised you had time for the morning chores."

"He's fun. I'm sure glad he came here. Aren't you?" Brenda went to the refrigerator for milk. "Iris? You aren't still mad at him, are you?" She touched Iris's arm.

"Of course I'm not mad at him, you silly girl. Why be unhappy about something you can't do anything about? Let's just say it's hard for me to get used to someone else making decisions around here, but the willow bends as the wind blows, or however that saying goes."

Brenda looked forlorn. "I don't think the saying goes like that."

Iris laughed. "You nut! Got any ideas about dessert for those hungry men who are having lunch here today?"

"How about that pound cake in the freezer? Thaw it and put some peaches and ice cream on it."

"Good thinking. Then I won't have to come in early to stick a frozen pie in the oven."

"I hate pound cake," Brenda admitted with a grin. "Let old Stanley eat it up and get rid of it."

Iris stooped and hugged her on her way to the freezer.

Though her heart was pounding in her breast, Iris tried not to act startled when she opened the door to the farrowing house and saw John hosing it down. He grinned at her and wrinkled his nose against the smell. The legs of his jeans were tucked into the tops of rubber boots. He was wearing a faded denim jacket, and on his head was a green-billed cap that advertised seed corn. She smiled as she watched him check the feeders while the hose ran fresh water into the trough. When she was sure she was in no danger of being sprayed with the hose, she went into the building and looked carefully at each of the big sows that lay dozing in the stalls.

"This one will be the first to farrow," she said when John came to lean on the rail beside her.

"Do you keep a chart on each of them?"

"I don't have that many. Dad was a grain farmer. I started this operation so we'd have a hog to butcher for quick money when we needed it. But the market has gone down. The money we get from the hogs today will go toward buying seed corn."

Iris was well aware, while they stood talking and watching the sow, that John's arm lay casually across her shoulders. She became so aware of it that she moved away. He seemed not to notice, and she was thankful.

The stockman, pulling a long hauling trailer behind his pickup, drove into the barnyard and backed up to the loading chute. Minutes later Stanley came driving in, slowly, as usual. Stanley never did anything in a hurry. He was a thickset man in his middle forties who for years had nurtured the hope of winning Iris . . . and the farm. Iris had already introduced John to the stock buyer when Stanley came ambling up to the three of them.

"Mornin', Iris."

"'Lo, Stanley. You know Mr. Waterfield. This is John Lang. Stanley Kratz lives down the road," she said, as if apologizing for his presence.

John held out his hand, and Stanley took it after a small hesitation. His eyes roamed suspiciously between Iris and John. "I heard you'd moved in here."

"You heard right," John said firmly, not in the least intimidated.

Alvin Hudson, whose farm bordered Iris's on the east, arrived. Iris had known Alvin and his wife, Ruth, all her life. They had been lifelong friends of her father's and had known her own mother briefly. If she needed a neighbor's help, she went to the Hudsons.

With two groups working, the hogs were rounded up and loaded, with the receipt in Iris's jacket pocket, in less than two hours. John and Alvin worked together, leaving Iris teamed with Stanley. After the trailer of squealing pigs left the barnyard, Alvin and John disappeared into the machine shed.

Iris drew off her work gloves and laid them on the

72

top of a post, then adjusted the red bandanna she had tied gypsy-style over her hair. She knew Stanley wouldn't leave until he had a chance to talk to her alone. Might as well get it over with, she thought, and wondered why she'd ever been so stupid as to go out with him. Lonely and bored had been her excuse then. Now it seemed a puny reason.

"Y'know people are talkin' about *him* moving in here." Stanley was as tactless as usual, Iris thought in disgust. As always when he was nervous, he had a toothpick stuck in the corner of his mouth, and it bobbed up and down as he talked.

"Has someone said something to you?"

"No. But they have to Ma. Why'd'ya let him do it?" Small, dark eyes glittered, and Iris could tell he was seething.

"I don't think that's any of your business, Stanley."

"None of my business?" he asked aggressively. "Y'know I planned on you'n me . . . gettin' together. I ain't gonna stand by and let that sonofabitch come in here and take over."

"Stanley! Calm down. You're making a fool of yourself. I've told you a thousand times there's absolutely no chance of you and me getting together . . . ever! I appreciate your friendship. You've been a good neighbor, but that's all!"

"Ain't good enough, is that it? Wal, I was plenty good enough when you needed help shelling corn and cuttin' pigs. I suppose you forgot that I planted beans for two whole days a couple years ago when you was stuck in the house with that sick kid. You've had the last bit of work out of me, Miss Uppity-up. Ya think you've got a stud bull here, but he won't stay, and you'll come crawling back for help. Wal, you won't get it from me." His anger caused his voice to tremble, and his jaw was rigid.

"You've always had a dirty mind," Iris said calmly. "That's only one of the things I despise about you. I wouldn't ask for your help again if I was drowning. Goodbye." She picked up her gloves and headed for the machine shed.

Stanley stood still for a moment, then stalked to his truck. Iris smiled when she heard the tires screech, throwing gravel. He'll run home and cry on his mama's shoulder. Yuk!

Alvin and John came out of the machine shed as she approached. Iris avoided John's eyes and smiled warmly at Alvin. His blue eyes twinkled, and his leathery face creased in a grin.

"What happened to Stanley? Is there a fire some-where?"

"Could be."

"I didn't think even a fire'd move Stanley that fast. What'd'ya do—tie a can to his tail?" Alvin was chuckling and scratching his gray head.

"Nothing as dramatic as that. How about some early lunch? I think it'll be dry enough to get in the field this afternoon."

"You don't have to feed me, gal."

"Sure, I do. Ruth expected you to stay, didn't she?

Just because we finished early is no reason for you not to."

"Wal, Mama did say something about going to town."

"Give me a few minutes and it'll be ready." Iris met John's eyes. There was no way she could keep from including him. "John . . . ?"

"You may be setting a precedent, you know."

Why was she so happy? she wondered as she hung her smelly chore coveralls on the porch hook. Usually a confrontation like the one with Stanley would leave her shaking like a leaf.

She washed her face and hands, smoothed her hair, and picked up lipstick to add a little color to her lips, but put it down again. Watch it, my girl. Put that on and you might as well mail him a letter telling him . . . What? She looked at herself closely in the mirror. Iris Ouverson, are you so naive as to let a few kisses from a handsome man rattle you? In the sophisticated world he comes from everyone kisses everyone else, she reasoned, then almost giggled. Well . . . maybe not in the Navy, and maybe not in the same way he kissed her.

Okay, farm gal, be cool, as Brenda would say, and don't get all revved up over a flirtation. But . . .

John! Nearly everywhere her thoughts wandered, he was there.

Five

John slipped easily into country life. He worked tire-lessly, putting in several more hours each day after Iris had driven the big green tractor to the shed to help Brenda with evening chores. That first night she had sent Brenda with a large bowl of stew to leave in his kitchen. He'd had the same stew for lunch, but Iris had reasoned he would be too tired to care about eating the same meal twice in one day. After that it had seemed natural to send over a part of a roast she had prepared in the crock pot during the day, or a por-tion of a casserole. Usually she could hear the putt-putt-putt of the tractor coming back a little before dark. He was up at dawn, refueling the tractors and tending to the sheep and hogs before Iris came out of the house.

Friday, the night of the play, Iris stayed in the field until a little over an hour before they had to leave. "We're going to be late," Brenda wailed.

"No, we're not." Iris left her work clothes on the porch and ran barefoot up to the bathroom.

"I'm so nervous I could chew my fingers off up to my elbows. What if I fall down on the stage? What if I forget my lines? Oh, why did I let you talk me into trying out for the darn play in the first place?"

"Don't blame me," Iris called over the sound of the running bath water. "You had a crush on Tim Pruitt at the time. That's why you tried out."

"I don't have a crush on him now. His breath stinks!"

Iris laughed and stepped into the tub. "Give him a breath mint."

"He's so dumb he wouldn't get the hint. Can I come in?" Brenda didn't wait for an answer, but pushed the door open. "Stacy Watts is having a slumber party for the girls in the cast. I don't know whether I want to go or not."

"Why not? Stacy's your best friend."

"If I fall on my face tonight, I won't go!" Brenda plunked herself down on the stool, her elbows on her knees and her chin in her palms.

"What's gotten into you, Brenda Ouverson? There's not a doubt in my mind that you'll be the best actress on that stage. Why, every play you've been in, every Christmas program, you've been just great. Even at Confirmation you were the best speaker. Reverend Peterson was amazed at how well you spoke, and I was congratulated by ever so many people. Humph! You may have butterflies in your stomach now, but the minute you get on your stage makeup, you'll be cool and collected, eager to perform, in fact."

"Do you really think so? I feel like I've got to throw up."

"Of course I think so. There won't be a mother or sister or anyone there any more proud than I'll be. You haven't let me or yourself down in fourteen years, you useless nuisance, and you won't this time."

"I love you, Iris." Thin young arms went about Iris's shoulders and a quick kiss was planted on her cheek.

"And I love you, squirt. Now, get out of here. I need to get dressed or I'll disgrace *you*."

Iris brushed her hair until it crackled and then pulled it straight back from her forehead without a part and coiled it into a bun on the back of her head. Carefully she applied her makeup and put on gold loop earrings. After spraying herself generously with scent she put on her hose and slender-heeled pumps. Her wardrobe was limited, but the one thing that she knew looked good on her was her teal-blue suit, with its pencil-slim skirt, and the burnt-rose blouse with the soft bow at the neck.

When she was completely dressed she surveyed herself in the full-length mirror attached to the inside of her closet door. Not one to realize she had the classic beauty of her Swedish ancestors, she looked at herself critically and saw a slender, quiet woman whose hair was blond and smooth, whose skin was flawless, and whose blue eyes looked bluer with the faint brushing of eye shadow and liner. She was delighted that her skirt was just the right length and she had no runs in her hose, not even a snag!

"Are you ready, Brenda? We'll buy a sandwich at the drive-in, if you like."

"I ate three mini-pizzas when I came home from school. Iris, what if I get on stage and throw up?"

"If you do, wait till Tim Pruitt tells you he's engaged to another woman. Everyone will think it's part of the script and will marvel at what a good actress you are."

"Oh, you're silly, Iris, just silly," Brenda said with a snort, but she smiled. "Is John coming?"

"I don't know. He hasn't said anything about it to me, and he's still in the field. What's the overnight case for?"

"I may stay at Stacy's. It's okay, isn't it?"

"Well, I guess so. But I'll have to talk to Jane first."

"Why d'ya have to talk to Stacy's mom? I'm almost fifteen." Brenda went down the steps two at a time. Iris followed slowly, trying to get accustomed to walking in the heels she seldom wore.

"You'll be fourteen for eight more months, my crazy little sister who wants to grow up so fast."

Iris backed the eight-year-old Chrysler out of the garage. The car was rarely used, had low mileage, and was in excellent condition. Brenda had gone through a stage when she nagged Iris to sell it and get something newer. Then one day a group of high-school boys had gathered around and admired it as it sat in the school parking lot. Now Brenda thought their "antique" was cool, and washed it down occasionally without grumbling too much.

The auditorium was almost full, and it was just a few minutes until curtain time, when Iris saw John come in the side door. As he gave his ticket to a student and collected a program, his eyes scanned the audience. Then he moved to stand along the wall with others waiting for more chairs to be brought in so they could be seated.

Watching John from her place between Alvin's wife

and Stacy's mother, Iris knew that hers were not the only eyes on him. The fact that he was a stranger in this community where almost everyone knew everyone else would be enough to attract notice, but added to that, he stood head and shoulders above most of the other men waiting in line. He was wearing a dark brown suit, a tan shirt, and a tie. Iris smiled. His hair had already begun to rebel against the hair-brush that had tried to smooth it, and was curling over onto his forehead. A warm, happy feeling started in the pit of her stomach and spread. He had promised Brenda that he would come, and he was here.

The houselights dimmed, and Iris nervously clutched at her purse. Let Brenda do well, she prayed silently. Let her be pleased with her performance. She sat rigid for the first few minutes Brenda was on stage, then relaxed and enjoyed the play. Her little sister went through her lines without missing a beat, and, as she had the curtain speech, Iris was sure the roar of applause that followed was all for Brenda.

Numerous curtain calls followed, and a bouquet of flowers was presented to Louise Hanley, the drama coach. When the audience began to file out, Iris and Jane Watts went backstage to congratulate their girls.

Brenda clutched a huge bunch of flowers. "Iris!" Her voice squeaked with excitement. "Look what John sent me! They're even bigger than old lady—" She broke off when Iris, laughing, put her fingers over Brenda's mouth. "He was here, wasn't he? I know I saw him . . . way in back." She leaned forward to whisper in her sister's ear. "I did good, didn't I?"

"You did great! You were the very best, just as I knew you'd be. Now, what are you going to do about the slumber party?"

"I'm going! Will you take my flowers home for me?" Without waiting for an answer, she shoved them at Iris.

"Jane said she'll bring you home in the morning. I'll be in the field, but you know your usual Saturday chores, and you'd better ride Sugar a little and get that colt used to the lead rope."

"I will. Oh, I will. Iris, I'm so happy. Do you think I could be a movie star?"

"Sure." Iris's eyes were filled with love and pride. "You're pretty enough and you're a good actress. 'Bye, now. Have a good time."

When Iris reached the end of the long hall she looked back in time to see Stanley coming down it. Beyond him Louise Hanley and Brenda stood talking to John. Iris saw him reach out and lay an arm over Brenda's shoulders in a gesture of affection. Then she noticed Stanley bearing down on her. She walked quickly through the door and out into the darkness, hoping she would be lucky enough to reach her car and drive away before he could catch her.

Out on the highway, Iris glanced at the flowers lying on the seat beside her. Did John know how much his thoughtful gesture had meant to a young girl who had depended solely on an older sister for love, guidance, and encouragement? There had never been a strong masculine figure in Brenda's life. It was no wonder she was impressed by him. Her own father had ignored her most of the time, seeing in her the lasting evidence of his own folly in marrying a girl he'd known for only a few weeks.

The growl in Iris's stomach reminded her she'd had nothing to eat since a peanut-butter sandwich at noon. She slowed the Chrysler as she approached a fast-food place, but drove on after looking at the crowded parking lot. When she turned off the highway and onto the graveled county road she noticed a car behind her. Would John be coming home so early?

Iris drove into the garage, turned off the lights, and picked up Brenda's flowers. With her bag over her shoulder, she got out of the car and pulled down the garage door just as car lights came up the drive. She groaned when she recognized Stanley's car. He stopped between her and the back door, so she was forced to stand and wait for him to roll down the window.

"How about going for a bite to eat?"

"No, thank you, Stanley." She added no excuses, and wasn't very civil at that.

"The kid's at the party at the Wattses', so what's keepin' you from comin'?" He turned off the motor.

"The fact that I don't want to go with you." She gave him a hard stare. "Excuse me."

Stanley turned off the headlights and got out of the car before she could reach the back door. She turned to face him.

"Are you still mad about what I said the other day?"

"No, I knew you had a narrow and dirty mind. You merely substantiated it. I don't care what you think, Stanley. Or what your mother thinks, for that matter. If you'll excuse me, I have more important things to do."

"Like what?"

"That's none of your damned business," she hissed. "Now, go!"

Stanley crossed his arms over his chest and rocked back on his heels. "You think you'll get rid of me before *he* comes. Then the two of you will have it nice and cozy without the kid, is that it?"

"Stanley, I've said it once and I'll say it again: you're disgusting."

"He ain't comin'." He waited to see her reaction to his words, and when she failed to act surprised he added, "He's out with Louise Hanley."

Iris merely shrugged.

"Louise is a hot little piece. Everybody knows it," he said slowly, enjoying every shocking word.

"You're crude! You're a crude man with your mind in the gutter. I wonder how I ever thought I could be friends with you. Now, if you don't mind, get out of here!"

"I mind. I know what's got into you. You think I'm not good enough now that there's bigger fish to fry. Wal, I'm not having no woman throw me over for some city dude who thinks he's a *gentleman* farmer. You're stupid, Iris. Just plain stupid! He ain't goin' to stay here for long. I've seen his kind before. He's just

83

like his father. Old lady Lang never knew where he'd land next. He'll play 'round with you, but—"

"That's enough! Keep your opinions to yourself and get the hell out of here." Iris flung open the screen door and fumbled to put the key in the lock.

"Bull! Who do you think you're talking to?" When Stanley grabbed her arm he knocked the flowers out of her hand. They fell to the ground. He lifted them with the toe of his shoe and sent them flying into the bushes beside the back porch.

"You . . . you bastard!" Iris was furious. She faced him like a spitting cat. "That does it! Get off my property, Stanley, and don't ever come back. Neighbor or no neighbor, stay the hell off my place!"

Stanley's face darkened, and his eyes turned hard and cruel. "You always thought you was just a mite better than other folks." His hand tightened on her arm and jerked her toward him.

"Let go of me, you buzzard bait, or—"

"Or you'll what? Seems to me like I got comin' a little bit of what you've been giving away. I ain't as much as had a kiss outta you, so I figure I'll collect now."

Iris was afraid. Stanley was stupid, unreasonable, and crude, but she'd never known him to be physically cruel. From the look on his face she knew he was capable of it now. When he lowered his head to kiss her, she brought the sharp heel of her shoe down on his instep.

"Yeow!" The sound of pain came from deep in his throat. "You bitch!"

Iris was mad and scared. She was also strong. She balled her fist and swung. The blow landed on the side of his face, but he didn't let go of her arm.

"Turn me loose, you . . . you overstuffed toad, or I'll scratch your eyes out!" She tried to stomp on his foot again, but he held her away from him. She lifted her foot to kick him but was hampered by the high-heeled shoes and lost her balance. He hauled her up close to him and tried to find her lips with his. Iris screamed as desperation took control of her. She struggled with every ounce of her strength to avoid the mouth seeking hers.

Neither of them heard the car drive into the carport in the grove, but both heard the angry shout just before John reached them.

"You sonofabitch!"

His fist connected with Stanley's jaw the instant he released his hold on Iris. Stanley stumbled back against the car, regained his balance, lowered his head, and charged. John stepped aside and hit him again. Stanley stumbled back, turned, and draped himself over the hood of the car, breathing hard. John swore viciously.

"Get the hell out of here or I'll beat you to a pulp!"

John stood waiting. Stanley took a handkerchief from his pocket and held it to his nose before he turned away.

"You haven't heard the last of this," he growled.

He stumbled around the car and jerked open the door. The dome light shone briefly on his bloody face.

"Neither have you," John said angrily. "You bother her again and I'll do more than bloody your nose. I'll break both your damned legs!"

"You can have her, but you ain't gettin' much!" Stanley shouted, and shot off down the drive without turning on his headlights.

Iris held onto the screen door. She didn't know if she could move. During the struggle she had turned her ankle, and pain was shooting up her leg to her knee. She blinked back tears of pain and humiliation. Her purse lay on the drive, and the flowers were nowhere in sight.

"Did he hurt you?"

"N-no, but I've lost the key." She stood on one foot and made no move to look for it.

"He *did* hurt you! The bastard!"

"I turned my ankle. I don't think I can bend over. The key's down there somewhere." She nodded toward the grass beside the step. Her voice was calm, but her insides were in a turmoil.

John squatted down and ran his hand along the ground. "I'll have to get a flashlight. Will you be okay? Do you want to sit down?"

"I'll be all right." Iris was trembling, but she made an effort to keep her voice steady.

While he was gone she eased off the high-heeled shoe and tried to put her weight on her injured foot. The pain ran up her leg like a sharp knife. "Ohhh . . . damn you, Stanley," she muttered. She couldn't afford to be laid up even for a day at this time of year!

John was back with the light and easily found the keys. "Can you move just a little, so I can open the door?"

"I . . . can hop if you'll help me take off this other darn shoe. This wouldn't have happened if I hadn't been wearing such high heels."

"That bad, huh?" John slid an arm beneath her knees and lifted her easily. Her arm went about his neck. "Open the door." His face was close, his voice low in her ear. Iris obeyed, her heart galloping like a race-horse. He angled their bodies through the door, and the screen slammed behind them. He carried her into the kitchen and stopped inside the door. "Can you find the light switch?" When she turned on the light, she looked directly into eyes just inches from hers. They were smiling. So was his mouth. "I'm sorry you've hurt your ankle, but I'm glad I had an excuse to hold you." The smile faded. "Is this the first time he's pulled a stunt like this?"

She nodded. "He's angry because I told him off the other day." She wanted to wrap both arms about his neck and lay her head on his shoulder. She couldn't remember ever being held like this.

"About my being here?"

"Partly. He's had his eye on me . . . and the farm for a while." It was embarrassing to talk about it. She shivered. "We went out to dinner a couple of times. He wasn't quite so repulsive then, and . . . I thought we could be friends."

John chuckled and rubbed his nose against her

cheek. Iris felt giddy. "You foolish woman! No single red-blooded man is going to want to be *friends* with you!" He set her down on a chair. "I'll take a look at that foot."

"John? . . ." Her voice sounded loud and breathless. "My purse is out there in the yard, and he . . . he kicked Brenda's flowers over in the bushes beside the house."

He swore. "My Lord! He got off easy!" John took the flashlight out of his hip pocket and went out through the door. When he returned he placed the flowers and her purse on the table beside her.

"Thank you. And thank you for sending Brenda the flowers. She was terribly excited. No one has ever given her flowers before."

"She told me. She did great, didn't she?" He stood beaming proudly down at her. "The little devil put on a good show!"

"She was pleased you were there."

Smiling blue eyes looked down into hers, and he squatted down beside her. "I looked for you."

She wanted to tell him that she had looked for him too, but she said nothing, feeling a sudden, over-whelming self-consciousness. She had to change the subject, and ran her hand down over her ankle, which was noticeably swollen. "Of all the damned luck! This couldn't have come at a worse time. We should start planting in a day or two."

"Don't worry. We will. Take off your stocking and I'll look at it. I have some elastic wrap over at the house we can use if there are no broken bones. If there are, it's the hospital for you."

"No! Nothing is broken. It's just a sprain."

"We'll soon see. Are you going to take off that stocking, or am I going to have to do it?" That endearing grin appeared again, and Iris had to look away from it.

"I'll do it, but you'll have to leave."

"Panty hose, huh? Think you can manage? I'll run over and get the wrap. Hey, is that your stomach growling or mine?" He straightened, looking awfully tall looming over the chair in which she sat.

"Mine has the bad habit of doing that, but I think this time it's yours. Didn't you have dinner either?"

"Didn't have time. After you're attended to, I'll scare up a bite to eat for us. I'll be back in a minute, so if you want privacy you'd better move fast."

As soon as he was gone, she stood on one foot and wiggled the panty hose down over her hips to her knees, sank down on the chair, and drew them off. Her ankle was rapidly changing color. She shrugged out of her suit jacket and hung it over the back of the chair. She was debating with herself about trying to hop to the sink to put the flowers in water, when John came back. He had changed into jeans, a soft plaid shirt, and sneakers.

He pulled up a chair, lifted her leg, and laid it across his lap. His obviously experienced fingers moved gently over the swollen ankle. He probed. Then, with his hand cupped beneath her foot, he moved the joint carefully.

89

Iris winced and clamped her lower lip between her teeth.

"No broken bones. It's a bad sprain. I'll wrap it, and you'll have to stay off it for a few days."

"Oh, but—"

"No buts. I've taken care of dozens of sprains during my hitch in the service. I'm a certified paramedic, ma'am. You're in good hands."

"Was that your line of work in the Navy?"

"No. I was a commander on a gun boat."

"Did you like it?"

"It was okay at the time. I like farming better."

She stared intently at him as he wrapped her ankle. His profile was sharply defined, his nose straight, his lips firm. What was he thinking? Had there been many women in his life? Had he been married? It would be wonderful to have a man like him to lean on. The thought sent a queer little shock through her body.

"What have you decided?" he asked.

His question caught her off guard.

"Never mind," he said quickly, his voice kind, but his expression stern. He lifted her leg off his lap and eased her foot down until her heel rested on the floor. "Your feet are cold. Where are your slippers? Better yet, I'll go ahead and turn on some lights, then carry you upstairs, and you can put on something more comfortable." He was gone before she could protest. When he returned he scooped her up in his arms.

"John! No! I'm too heavy."

"Put your arms around my neck and you'll be light as a feather."

"I doubt that!" She felt protected and young. Almost cherished. An absolutely new and infinitely wonderful feeling to her.

"Hang on, or I'll drop you," he threatened. Her arms tightened, and it brought her face nearer his. The scent of his skin was dearly familiar.

"Let me walk, John. You can't carry me up those steps."

"Want to bet? What do you weigh? I'd say about one-twenty. Right?" She nodded. "Then, be still." He was breathing hard when they reached her room and he set her down on the edge of the bed. "Nicest workout I've had in a long time. Now, don't put your weight on that foot. Is there anything you can't reach with a few hops?"

"No. I can manage, thank you." The tightness in her chest increased with alarming intensity.

He leaned against the end of the heavy oak bed. "I never knew there were women like you, Iris." He said it as if she were something incredible. His eyes circled the utterly feminine room, with its deep-ruffled criss-cross curtains, pale blue carpet, and frilly lampshades, coming back to look hard at her. "You were badly frightened by Stanley. I heard your scream. How come you didn't have hysterics afterwards?" His straight-forward stare did more than Stanley's attack to unnerve her.

"I . . . don't know. I guess I'm not the hysterical type." She avoided his eyes, and lifted her hands to tuck stray strands of hair into the bun.

He walked around to stand by the edge of the bed in front of her, and she had to look up a long way to see his face. "You and Brenda have lived here alone for five years?" She nodded, and he said, "Amazing!" He moved about the room, touched a picture of her and Brenda taken when she first came home from college, lifted a brush on the bureau, glanced at a stack of books on the table beside the bed. He turned and gave her a meaningful look. "Do you like grilled-cheese sandwiches?"

Iris let the air out of her lungs with one big puff and chuckled. "Love 'em."

"Good." She hadn't realized quite how serious his expression had been, until he smiled. It made all the difference. "I make the best grilled-cheese sandwich in the West," he bragged. "Do what you have to do, then yell. I'll come get you." At the door his eyes caught hers and held them. "I have got a bottle of wine I've been saving for a special occasion. I think this is it." The twinkle in his eyes matched the grin on his lips. "By the way, why does Arthur have to stay in the barn at night?"

"You know one of the reasons." Her eyes twinkled back at him.

He cocked his head to one side and studied her.

"Oh, yes. I intend to have a talk with you about that." He winked, turned, and moved out of sight with swift grace.

She sat for a long time, fervently wishing for many impossibilities, all involving John D. Lang, Jr.

Six

Iris stood at the head of the stairs, her leg trembling from the effort it took to hop down the hall. She knew she could make it down the steps by taking them one at a time and leaning on the smooth oak rail, but first she needed rest. She had slipped into the new caftan she'd made during the winter; one of the soft feminine types of things she liked to wear after supper. The blue material, with a Victorian print, was soft cotton; the fabric had caught her eye at a warehouse sale where prices were slashed drastically. She could never have afforded it otherwise. Usually in the evening she let her hair hang loose, but tonight, recalling John's remark about Lady Godiva, she coiled the braid and pinned it to the back of her head.

She took the steps slowly. The seldom-used ceiling light in the dining room was on. Just like Brenda, she mused. Doesn't know the meaning of the word "economize." At the bottom of the stairs she wrapped her arms around the newel post to steady herself and to give her pounding heart time to slow down.

"What the devil are you doing down here? You stubborn little jackass!" John's long strides brought him quickly to her, and he scooped her up in his arms. He lifted her high, and her arms automatically went around his neck. "What are you trying to do to me? Don't you want me to have any fun?" He started for

93

the kitchen and stopped. He lowered his head and nuzzled the soft skin of her neck. "I like this." His voice was slightly husky, his face inches from hers. "You're the damndest woman I've ever known. You can go from a tomboy chasing hogs, to looking chic like you did tonight at the school, to soft and womanly like now." His eyes looked into hers for a long, delicious moment, and tides of overwhelming warmth washed over her. "I like this Iris the best." The words came out on a soft breath.

"I'm a complete package," she whispered. Before she could think of something flip to say, he bent his head and kissed her softly.

"Sure, you are. Ready for the party?" He carried her into the kitchen and stood her beside the table, his arm supporting her. "Sit here, ma'am. Dinner will be served in a minute."

The table held two place settings, catsup, and steak sauce. "I thought we were having grilled-cheese sandwiches."

"A minor problem developed."

"What was that?"

"No cheese." He stirred frozen hash-browns, poked at two small steaks in another pan. "I'll bring you a glass of wine in a minute."

"I don't like sitting here doing nothing."

"You're entitled to be pampered once in a while, so relax and enjoy it. Besides, you have the perfect excuse tonight—you're an invalid, remember?"

She nodded, smiling happily. After a glass of wine

and then some hot food, she decided being pampered was definitely nice!

"Mmmm . . . that was good," she said when she finished her steak. "Where did you learn to cook?"

"Not aboard ship. I knew how to cook when I went into the Navy. I more or less shifted for myself during my school years, and it was cook or live on cold cereal." He filled her wineglass. "We may as well kill the bottle." She thought his eyes were the most beautiful eyes she'd ever seen. "I can just see the wheels turning in your mind. You're thinking that I'm plying you with drink so I can seduce you."

"Are you?"

"Yeah. Just in case the mating salt I sprinkled on the potatoes doesn't work." He gave her one of his wide, winning grins.

She couldn't hold back her own smile in spite of the warmth from embarrassment that flooded her face. "C'mon, be serious. What kind of childhood did you have?"

"My parents were divorced. My mother worked, and I was on my own a lot. But it was okay. How about yours?"

"Mine was okay, too. After my mother died I had my grandma, than an aunt, and my dad. I always had a horse and a dog. It was a good childhood."

"I saw you on your horse one time when I was here visiting my grandmother. You had long blond pigtails hanging down your back. You were maybe fifteen or sixteen. My granny told me to stay away from you, that you were a pure, sweet girl." The look on his face made her breathless. "Granny was right."

Iris sipped her wine and tried not to look at him. Her face began to feel warm again. The intensity of his gaze made her uncomfortable. She picked up the soiled plates and stacked them.

"Brenda will wash the dishes in the morning. One of her Saturday chores," she explained with a short laugh.

John took the dishes out of her hands. "Is this your way of telling me the party is over?" His grin spread that horrible charm over his face. "I was taught that it was rude to eat and run." He cleared the table and rinsed the dishes, stacking them neatly in the sink. He turned to face her, grinning still. "How will you get up the stairs without me?"

"I'll walk. I've been putting a little pressure on my ankle while sitting here, and discovered it isn't that bad." She limped to the counter and back to the table to demonstrate.

John flipped off the overhead light, making the room rosy with only the dim light from over the stove. She turned away. "Do you want me to go?" He was close behind her, his voice almost a whisper, when he repeated the question. "Do you want me to go, Iris?"

She nodded. "I think you should." It was hard for her to say anything.

"You think I want to make love to you. Is that it?"

"No . . . I just think—"

"You're wrong. I want to make love to you very

much. I've wanted to since the first time I saw you. Since the very first," he whispered once more, his face near hers, his hands on her shoulders drawing her to his chest.

When she lurched away from him, his hands fell from her shoulders. She went slowly into the dining room, scarcely noticing the pain in her ankle. Her hand found the switch beside the door and clicked off the overhead light. In the gloom the familiar room seemed strange. The feelings stirring inside her were even stranger, and she was frightened by them. She wrapped her arms about the post at the foot of the stairs and rested her chin on the smooth, rounded top. She fought to overcome her inhibitions while the need to be held and caressed blazed fiercely through her.

"Iris?" John's gentle hands pulled her around to face him. Every bone in her body seemed to have turned to jelly. She made not a whimper of protest when his arms closed about her, merely lifting her parted lips for his kiss. His mouth was warm and gentle and gave her room to move away if she wanted to. She found herself clinging to him weakly. His hands moved seductively across her hips and back, tucking her closer to the granite strength of his body. Her mind felt like it was floating. Primitive desire grew inside her, and she became helpless to stop it. These wanton feelings were new and strange to her, and instead of making an effort to control them, she allowed them to take over, to build into sexual intoxication.

It was John who drew back and held her away from him.

"I don't sleep around," she gasped. Oh, dear Lord! That surely was an understatement. Would he be amused to know she'd never been with a man before? Her arms fell from around him.

"I know that." He lifted first one of her arms and then the other and placed them about his neck. He pressed a sweet kiss to her moist parted lips before his mouth trailed to her ear. "I'm going to take the pins out of your hair." Warm fingers smoothed back the strands from her temples on their way to the back of her head. "I've been wanting to see it again since that first night. Why were you angry when I called you Lady Godiva?" Her forehead was pressed to his shoulder and his whispered words floated around her. "In some parts of the world a man cherishes his woman's hair." He unlaced the braid, and his hands caressed the glossy strands that hung past her waist. "You're a treasure, a rare flower, my Iris." He continued to stroke her from the crown of her head to her hips.

Mindless, unconscious of time or place, Iris leaned on him. "I've cut it only one time." It seemed an inconsequential thing to say with her lips against his neck.

The hands on her shoulders moved her back, and he tilted her face with fingers beneath her chin. Her arms fell to her sides. She felt scared . . . and shy. But his face was soft with charm and his eyes moved over her warmly. He took two handfuls of hair and brought the silky strands forward over her shoulders and smoothed them down over her breasts. "It would be a crime to cut it," he said, almost to himself. "I've always had a yearning to see an old-fashioned girl with long golden hair."

He drew her gently to him, and his lips settled on her mouth with infinite passion and tenderness. His tongue made small forays between her lips before it entered her mouth and searched for sweetness. His hands traversed her body. Her mouth blossomed under his. Instinctively she responded by welcoming the invasion of his tongue and moved her own to gently stroke his inner lips. Her fingers moved to the hair at the back of his neck, spread, and boldly combed and caressed.

His hands gripped the soft flesh of her hips, pressing her soft mound against his arousal. Abruptly his lips were at her ear and he was taking deep breaths.

"Tell me to stop . . . to go home, or it'll be too late." The words seemed wrenched from him. "I . . . ache for you. . . ."

She wanted to speak, to tell him she was still a girl in a woman's body, that she was afraid of the hurt that would follow this giving of herself. She opened her mouth to whisper her fears, but it was too late. He covered her parted lips, his tongue darting hotly in and out of her mouth, exploring every curve of the sweetness that trembled beneath his demanding kiss. Her arms tightened while he ravaged the sweetness of her until she was moaning gently and panting for breath. She kissed him back feverishly, as though swept away by some wild force totally beyond her control.

In a small part of her mind she realized this was what she wanted, had wanted since the first time he kissed her. It was as though it was his right, and she had waited for him. Now, she would know exactly what it was that she had been waiting for. She would learn the mysteries about which she had read and imagined but never truly believed were accompanied by such overwhelmingly forceful feelings. He was almost a stranger to her, his background as different from hers as night from day, she thought frantically. And yet she felt as though she'd known him all her life, wanted him, needed him, loved him. . . .

"Let's go upstairs," he whispered urgently.

Iris shuddered, feeling as though her legs were too weak to hold her without his supporting arms. She knew she should have been shocked by his suggestion, but she wasn't, for his husky whisper aroused her on some instinctive level long suppressed that was rushing to take control of her virgin body. "Turn out all the lights down here." It was a mere fragment of a whisper from her aching throat.

"Can you make it up the steps alone?"

Even now, his concern was for her, and she cherished it. She nodded, and the cheek pressed tightly against his felt the pull of a day's growth of beard.

Reluctantly, it seemed, his arms fell away from her.

His hands at her waist assisted her up the first step and then he left her.

I do love him! she thought wildly. I wouldn't be going to bed with him if I didn't! Oh, dear heaven! It's unreal that I'm doing this.

The light from the yard dimly lit the room. Iris stood at the foot of the bed she had slept in for most of her life. Her face burned, and her stomach muscles clenched and relaxed. Her breathing and heartbeat were all mixed up, as if a motor had been attached to them and their normal rhythm had gone awry. It seemed to her that she stood there for an eternity.

Then he was behind her. He hadn't touched her, but she knew. She leaned back against him. She needed his strength, his assurance. His large, warm hands came around her, circled her rib cage, and pulled her back against his chest. His mouth found the curve of her neck, lips nibbling, his breath tantalizing her skin. She turned in his arms. He had removed his shirt, and she wrapped her arms about his naked torso. Her ragged breath was trapped inside her mouth by his plundering lips, and the floor seemed to fall away at her feet.

"I shouldn't!" she whispered urgently when his lips left hers to gulp air. Ingrained teaching of moral standards surfaced to plague her even now.

"Yes!" he whispered hoarsely. "You're a woman made to be loved and . . . cherished." His hungry mouth searched, found hers, and held it with fierce possession. His hands moved urgently over her. "How do I get you out of this thing?"

"Zipper . . . in back."

Woosh! She felt the air on her bare skin as the caftan fell in a soft pool around her feet. She backed away from him and sat down on the bed. In one swift flick she rid herself of her slippers, then she slid swiftly between the sheets. Her eyes were riveted on John's tall and shadowy figure, motionless before her. When his hands went to the belt of his jeans, she closed her eyes, and sweet warmth washed over her.

The bed sagged. She could feel his body just beyond her hip. He sat on the edge of the bed for what seemed only an instant before the covers lifted and she felt long, hair-roughened legs against her and arms that seemed to be yards long scooping under and around her. She was gathered tenderly to a warm naked chest thickly matted with soft hair.

He pinned the length of her against him and cradled her head in the crook of his arm. She couldn't move, didn't want to move, and felt as if her heart would gallop right out of her breast.

"Are you shy with me?" he whispered between kisses around her ear. "Don't be. You're beautiful. Your body is strong and neat. It's like velvet, soft, and yet firm and tight. And this wonderful hair . . ." His fingers fumbled with the hooks on her bra, then swept it from her breasts. For the first time, her nipples were pressed against a man's chest. His hand pushed at the panties, and she lifted her hips to help him.

Her palms slid over muscle and tight flesh as if wanting to know every inch of him. So this was what it was like to make love, she thought dreamily, and threaded her legs between his. His sex was large and firm, and throbbed against her flat stomach. She gloried in the feel of him, knowing that soon he would fill that aching emptiness. Her hands moved caressingly up and down his side and over his hips to the small of his back.

His breath came in quick gasps, and he turned her on her back so he could hover over her. He lowered his head and kissed her breast. His tongue flicked the bud, then grasped it gently with his teeth. He nuzzled the soft mound like a baby seeking life-giving substance. His hand moved over her body, prowling ever closer to the ultimate goal, and suddenly it was there at the mysterious moistness. Her legs opened for him.

Tremors shot through her in earth-shaking waves as exploring fingers moved, titillating the pulsing flower of womanhood, until her hips arched frantically against the hand between her legs and she instinctively reached for the male hardness to fill her. She was in a mindless void where there were only John's hands, John's lips, John's body. Her hand circled him and pulled, her knees flexed. She could feel him tremble violently as he slid between her thighs and held himself poised above her. He sought the warm cavern and entered.

Iris gave a small strangled cry. He stopped and lay

motionless atop her. The two hands that cupped her hips squeezed, released, and squeezed again.

"Oh, baby! Why didn't you tell me?" He groaned hoarsely against the side of her face.

She turned her head, frantically seeking his lips. "Don't stop!" It was a quavering whimper.

"I can't . . . stop! But, sweetheart . . . darling . . . Oh, God!"

He raised himself. She thought he was going to leave her, and grabbed frantically at his lean hips. He paused, then pierced her savagely with a single, jarring thrust. A stab of white-hot pain forced a choked cry from her lips. A low moan came from his. He supported himself on his forearms, tangled his hands in her hair, and rained feverish kisses on her face.

For a while he remained motionless, allowing her to become accustomed to the feel of him inside her, while his lips searched out every line in her face and sipped at the tears that rolled from the corners of her eyes. Then, slowly, he started to move within her, thrusting carefully. Her arms wound tightly around his back, feeling his muscles strain and stir beneath her palms when he plunged faster and faster. The naked hunger that caught her was both sweet and violent. Every part of him that touched her carried a fiery message to the depth of her femininity, and her hips moved with the surging rhythm of his. He was quivering with the effort to love her tenderly. His heart thundered against her breast. It surprised her that she could feel it over the hammering of her own.

When she thought she would explode, when the pain-pleasure became so intense, she drew his tongue into her mouth. Then she did explode within. The first fantastic sensation was closely followed by another and then another. As she emerged from a long, unbelievable release she was aware of nothing but a wonderful floating feeling and the broad naked shoulders she clung to until the world stopped tilting.

Almost simultaneously, John thrust into her for the last time, his whole body tense with emotion for wild exhilarating seconds. He gripped her fiercely, and the air exploded from his lungs. Then he was still.

Iris lay weak and limp beneath him; her body seemed lifeless even though her heart still beat too quickly in her breast and her blood raced through her veins.

Seemingly awed into silence by the experience they'd shared, John slid to her side and gathered her gently to him.

"Sweetheart . . ." He smoothed her hair back from her damp face and spread it out on the pillow behind her head. "Oh, love!" He placed soft kisses on her forehead, her eyes. "I never imagined that you were . . . were a virgin. I didn't want to be rough, to hurt you, but I was so hungry for you I couldn't help myself." His hand moved down her side to her bottom and then to her thigh and pulled it up so it rested across his. His hand returned to caress the soft rounded flesh of her hips.

"I'm sorry." She said it so low he could scarcely

hear, but he did, and he moved his face back so he could see her. Her eyes were closed. He felt a tear drop on his shoulder.

A low growl of protest came from his throat. "Why are you crying? Are you sorry you didn't save yourself for the man you love?"

"No. I wanted it to be you. I'm sorry if you were disappointed."

"Disappointed?" he muttered thickly. "Sweetheart, didn't you know that it's a treasured moment in a man's life when he presses against that barrier? He knows that no man has been there before him and for the rest of her life a woman will remember him." He kissed away the tears. "How can you possibly think I was disappointed? I shall cherish the memory of this night always." His hand moved soothingly over her back in a gentle rhythm. He whispered words of comfort and kissed away the moistness on her face.

Relaxed and dreamy, she listened to the steady beat of his heart beneath her cheek and marveled that his hard muscles and angled frame could provide such a comfortable resting place.

"I suppose you've known many women," she said, not really wanting to know about the women in his life.

"A few. But none the way I know you."

"You mean I'm the only thirty-two-year-old virgin you've slept with?" The words were out of her mouth even while she was thinking them.

The hand on her back came up to cover her cheek and press her face to his chest. "Don't talk about it like that. You're the first real, complete woman I've been with." His voice was deeply sincere.

Her palm slid up his chest to his face and stroked it lovingly. "Your lovemaking is better than anything I've read in a book," she confessed shyly.

He laughed and rolled with her in his arms, her hair covering them. She giggled and clutched at him to keep from falling off the bed.

"This is only the beginning, my beautiful innocent," he said, and wrapped her hair around his shoulders.

"You're the teacher," she said saucily, and boldly nipped him on the chin, then sweetly kissed the spot.

"Will you sign up for the full course?"

"What's the tuition? How many credits? And what are the job opportunities when I graduate?"

He roared with laughter and rolled with her again. They both almost toppled to the floor, only his foot braced against the carpet saving them. On top of him, Iris grabbed at the headboard to keep from falling.

"Stop that!" She laughed, her belly pressed tightly to his. "We're too big for this bed."

He was suddenly still, his foot on the floor, his other leg wrapped over hers. Her hair covered their upper bodies.

"I could feel your laugh," he whispered. "It's truly youthful and innocent. How did you manage to escape the perniciousness of our generation?" She lifted her head to look at him, but he lifted his and caught her lips. Her head followed his down, and they shared a deep, hungry kiss.

It was an exhilarating experience to be in control. Iris felt his heartbeat soar. She angled her nose alongside his and caressed his lips with her own, nibbling, stroking with her tongue, deepening the kiss and withdrawing. She felt and tasted the moistness of his skin. All the adoration she had saved was given to him now. She murmured his name as her lips glided over straight brows, short, thick eyelashes, cheeks rough with stubble, and to his waiting mouth. It was glorious to feel this freedom to love and caress him. Awed by the wonder of it, she paused and pressed her cheek to his.

"Ah, love! Don't stop!" His voice came huskily, tickling her ear. His hands kneaded her rounded bottom and pressed her tightly to the aroused length of him, captured between their bellies. "I've been in a bad way since I've been here; all those nights of wanting you . . ." His leg glided from over hers, and his hand moved to spread her thighs. He lifted her with strong thumbs pressed to her hipbones. When he settled her on him, she gasped with surprise. "Just be still, sweetheart. I won't hurt you." His hands glided over her hips and back and up to the sides of her breasts, which were flattened against his chest. He grasped her head and turned it so his lips could reach her mouth. "We fit perfectly, love," he said, breathing deeply. "We're perfect together." His voice was a shivering whisper that touched her soul.

Much later, as she lay quietly beside him, he turned and buried his face in the curve of her neck like a child seeking comfort. Time and again he had told her how he liked to feel her hair around his shoulders. She covered him with it and stroked his own back from his forehead, loving him, wanting him to love her in return but realizing how improbable it was. She tried to dismiss the feeling of impending heart-ache. In torment she tightened her arms around him and pressed her mouth to his forehead. Finally she fell asleep, wishing the night wouldn't pass so quickly.

It seemed she had scarcely closed her eyes when a loud noise awakened her. Someone was banging on the door. Shouts followed.

"Fire! Fire!"

Seven

Fire! The word caused an icy ball of fear to knot in the pit of Iris's stomach.

John untangled his limbs from hers and jumped out of bed. He slid into his jeans without benefit of underwear and was pulling them up around his hips as he vaulted out of the bedroom door. The shouts from the yard below and the hammering on the door were persistent.

Iris, forgetting her sprained ankle, cried out when she slammed it against the table as she hurried to slide a robe over her head. She grabbed her shoes and limped at a run after John.

"Barn's on fire!" The shout came through the opened door.

"Iris, call the fire department!" John shouted, and raced back up the steps. He returned with his shoes in his hand as she dialed the number.

Iris carried the phone to the window. Flames were shooting from the roof of the barn. She forced herself to be calm and give directions to the radio operator, who would notify the volunteer firemen.

"Please hurry," she pleaded before she slammed down the phone.

The horror of it really struck her when she limped out the door. Angry flames leaped from the top of the barn, lighting the sky.

"Oh, my God! The animals!"

As if watching a movie, she saw John racing toward the barn. He opened the door and Arthur shot out. She ran in after John.

"Get out of here!" he shouted.

"The horses—"

"I'll get 'em!"

Iris could hear the whinnies of the frightened animals. Disregarding John's order, she ran down the aisle to Sugar's stall, flung it open, and stepped aside as the horse plunged past her, the colt at her heels. Smoke choked her. Burning embers fell into the corridor. The roaring fire was consuming the hay in the loft.

She knew John had reached the west stalls when a frightened horse charged down the aisle. She flattened herself against the railing so she wouldn't be trampled.

One more. She could hear Buck's piercing shrieks of terror and John's bellows as he tried to turn the crazed animal. She ran to the end of the barn. The smoke was thicker here. John didn't see her. He had pushed open the gate thinking the horse would follow him out.

Buck was rearing in his stall, striking futilely at the bars. The gate had swung in instead of out, and the animal was confused.

"Buck! Buck!" Somehow the horse heard her through his terror and over the roar of the fire. She flung the gate open wide, and he plunged through.

She pulled the collar of her robe over her nose so she could breathe, and felt her way along the stalls to the door. John grabbed her and hauled her outside. Gasping for breath, she barely heard him cursing her.

"Damn you! You scared the hell out of me!" He glared down at her. Light from the flames flickered over his naked chest. "Get that hair under your robe! A spark could land on it!"

There was mass confusion. The horses, hogs, and sheep, all frightened, darted around. Arthur ran and barked at the sows, whose heavy bellies made them flounder as they tried to get away from him. The wind was sending burning embers into the yard, adding to the terror of the animals and people there.

"Are the animals out?" a man called.

Iris blinked, barely able to recognize the speaker as Mr. Downs, whose farm was just down the road. His clothes were muddy from the hog pen, and he'd lost his hat. She couldn't remember ever seeing him without that hat.

"All the animals are out!" John called back, his voice hoarse. "The machinery! Help me get it out of the shed. In this wind everything could go!" He took off at a run. "Get the cars, Iris," he shouted over his shoulder.

Iris ran to the house for the keys. Her ankle throbbed with every step. She backed the pickup out toward the grove and then returned for the Chrysler. The robe flopped around her legs and the naked body beneath it shivered, but not from cold . . . from fear.

All the lights on the farm went out. The flames had reached the fuse box. The area was illuminated now by the fire, and the heat scorched her face. Only then did the enormity of what was happening hit her. The barn! The eighty-year-old barn her grandfather had built and all the other buildings, too, were burning!

In all her life, Iris had never felt so helpless. The wind seemed to take vengeance, sending the hungry flames higher, fanning them toward the oak tree that spanned the drive. She paused and stared in numbed disbelief, scarcely noticing the car careening into the yard.

"What can we do?" Young Jerry, a friend of Brenda's, grabbed her arm.

"The tack house!" she gasped. "Brenda's saddle is in

112

the tack house!" Two other boys darted past her. "Be careful," she called. "Jerry, help me get things out of the garage—"

The yard was full of neighbors before the shrill sound of the fire-truck whistle announced its arrival. They were too late! Too late! The thought pounded at Iris as she watched the fire spread to the tack house, the garage, and finally the machine shed, where people were helping John put as many small pieces as they could into the loader on the tractor.

The red light on top of the fire truck spun round and round, giving the area an even more eerie appearance. Most of the people standing on the lawn had coats over nightgowns and pajamas. News of a fire spread fast in this small community, where most people had fire and police radios.

The volunteer firemen attached the hose to the water wagon and turned it on the oak tree. The oak tree! The top was blazing and dropping burning branches onto the roof of the house. Oh, God! No! Iris froze. Then John was shaking her arm.

"Go shut the windows. They'll have to wet down the roof." She stood there. "Iris! Go! The flashlight is on the kitchen counter. And . . . put on some clothes." He pushed her toward the door.

Later Iris was to wonder how she managed to get through the early-morning hours. Mr. Downs had spotted the fire at 3:00 A.M. on his way home from Des Moines. Before daylight every building on the farm had burned to the ground, with the exception of

113

the house, and it had suffered roof damage. Iris stood among the lilac bushes that lined the lower drive. Tears streamed down her face. In all her life she'd never known such crushing defeat. Not only was her farm in shambles, but so was her reputation. Unaware that Iris was standing in the shadows, her neighbors gossiped about her. The crowd that gathered to watch the fire was buzzing with the news that Mr. Downs had tried to rouse John Lang, because the lights were on in the trailer house. When that failed he pounded on Iris's door and John came out of the house pulling on his pants. Crude laughter followed the telling of the story.

"Not a very good example to set for Brenda . . . He didn't waste any time . . . But why should he, when she was here and available? . . . I'm surprised at Iris; I never thought of her as being *that* kind of woman . . . You can't tell about the cool, silent types . . . Look at her old man, he took that young girl . . . got her pregnant . . . He married her, though; that's more than this guy'll do . . . I know his type . . . get it while you can!" Snickers followed the remarks. Iris moved away, blinded by tears, her heart as heavy as lead. Being ridiculed by the people she had known all her life cut her to the quick.

Jane Watts brought Brenda home just as dawn was lighting the eastern sky. "We just heard . . . Jerry called."

Brenda looked with horror at what had happened to her home. She burst into tears and threw herself into

114

her sister's arms. Iris tried to comfort her, but the sobs issuing from her own throat only made Brenda cry harder. At last, Iris was able to get a grip on her emotions. "Sugar and the colt are fine," she said. "You'll have to round them up today. We just turned them loose. The boys got your saddle out of the tack house, and the spare bridles, too. They even carried out that green wooden chest of yours with the old Civil War stirrup in it." Iris's tears mingled with those of her sister. They clung together. Things they had known and lived with all their lives were gone.

"The rabbits?" Brenda choked, swallowed, and repeated. "Did you get the rabbits out? Are Elizabeth and her babies all right?"

"Mr. Downs opened all the cages. We'll have to hunt for them. They were scared, and heaven knows where they are now."

"How did it happen? What started it?" Brenda asked the question that had, plagued Iris throughout the long hours.

"We don't know. The fire chief said it must have started in the loft and ignited the hay. That's the reason it spread so rapidly. The wiring was old, but we've always been careful not to overload the circuits."

The spectators drifted away until only the firemen were left. They sprayed the blackened ruins in shifts. Ruth and Alvin brought coffee and sandwiches and passed them out to the tired men. John stood among them. He'd found time to put on a sweat shirt. He seemed like a stranger to Iris now. She kept thoughts of what had happened between them from her mind and prayed that Brenda wouldn't hear the gossip. If she did, Iris hoped she'd be able to find the words to explain her actions.

The sun came up. For the first time Iris had a view of the fields behind the barn from the kitchen window. The blackened ruins stood out in bold relief. Wisps of smoke still curled up from deep in the bowels of the rubble. The fire trucks went back to town, and Alvin and Ruth departed. Only the fire chiefs car remained. He and his assistant were writing on a pad and talking to John. The three men came toward the house, and Iris went out to meet them on the back step.

"It was overloaded wires, Miss Ouverson. There's no doubt about it. That old wiring is dangerous. The wire they put in that barn fifty years ago didn't carry much insulation."

"I knew the wiring was old. Brenda and I never used anything but a forty-watt bulb in the barn." Iris blinked back tears. She couldn't cry in front of these men!

"There was an extension run to the hog house," the chief said, scratching his head with the pencil. "I don't know exactly where it was plugged in."

"I plugged it into the socket that hung down nearest the south window," John said.

"Then that's what did it. I figure the fire started in the loft in the southwest corner."

"I had no idea . . ." John's eyes went from the fireman to Iris's frozen face.

She couldn't utter a word except a muted "thank you" to the fireman when he left.

"Iris . . ."

She stood absolutely still, while all the color drained from her face. Against the pallor, her eyes were dark with hurt.

"If I was responsible, I'm sorry."

She ignored the pleading look in his eyes, while tears welled up in hers. "If? . . ." she choked on the word, then turned on her heel and left him.

Her hands gripped the edge of the kitchen sink. Pain knifed through her head and settled behind her eyes. She closed them and rocked back and forth in her misery. She was deep in the pit of despair. Then *his* hands were on her shoulders. She shrugged them off and stood there. Distress made her body wooden. He touched her again.

"Don't!"

"Look at me, for crissake! How do you think I feel?"

"I don't give a damn how you feel! Get away from me. Get out of this house!" A storm of words broke from her lips. "You think you know so much! Did you learn how to burn down my barn in those books? Didn't it occur to you to ask about running the extension? Or to wonder why I didn't burn a light in the hog house?" she added bitterly.

"No, it didn't occur to me. I wouldn't have had this happen for anything. Iris—"

She whirled. Her eyes blazed into his. "Your stupidity has erased forever a landmark that's stood for eighty years. Live with that while you're wondering whether or not to sell that livestock running loose out there because there's nothing to feed them. And what are you going to do for seed corn, Mr. Smart Alec? There isn't enough money in the farm account to buy more."

"What about insurance?"

"What about it? Do you think the policy will build another barn with hand-hewed oak beams? Ha! Maybe the insurance money will cover a prefabricated tin building half the size of our beautiful old barn." Rage and the blinding headache were making her sick to her stomach. "Get out your checkbook, Mr. Moneybags. You've won. It's all yours!"

She brushed past him and headed for the stairs. In her room the tight reins she had held on her facial muscles broke, and she crumpled. She threw herself on the bed and gave way to a flood of tears.

Iris woke to a thousand drums beating in her head. The pain was so intense she couldn't focus her eyes. Her stomach heaved. She staggered to the bathroom and leaned over the commode. Convulsions racked her, leaving her feeling as if her head was being squeezed in a vise. As soon as she could stand, she got the headache pills out of the medicine cabinet, took one with a sip of water, and immediately threw it up. She cried with frustration. Knowing it was useless to try again, she clutched the bottle in her hand and stumbled down the hall. She fell into bed and pulled the covers over her head. She didn't have the strength to lower the shades.

Sometime later she vaguely realized her head was being lifted and a glass was placed to her lips. She swallowed so she would be left alone, and sank again in a sea of pain. Sleep, stirring dreams. Pain and despair beyond tears. Blessed darkness. She floated in black clouds, helpless and lonely. She cried, but there were no tears.

When she awakened, her vision was blurred by pain and exhaustion. It was evening. She didn't know how she knew, but it was. Slowly memory returned, and the sounds recorded in her mind drummed in her ears. The roar of the fire, the siren, the whinnies of the frightened horses, the neighbors' voices. *I didn't know she was that kind of woman.* John was responsible for everything.

She didn't want to get up. Not now. And no more tears. Crying was a foolish waste of energy. She had to think. She turned her head carefully and looked at the ceiling. Pain still throbbed behind her eyes, but she wasn't nauseated. A glass of water and the prescription bottle sat on the nightstand. She took one of the tablets and drank the full glass of water. Nothing seemed important. She lay back and folded her arms over the top of her head. She closed her eyes and drifted to sleep again.

When she opened them, John stood beside the bed looking down at her. For a long moment they stared at each other. Smoky gray eyes stared solemnly up at him. The ache in her chest left no room for any feeling for him.

"How do you feel?"

"All right." A kind of brittle calm possessed her. "Can I get you something? More water?"

"No. You can get out of my room, out of my house." She rolled her head toward the wall so she wouldn't have to look at him.

"I realize you're depressed over losing the buildings," he said quietly. "But you could've lost more. The house, the machinery."

She turned her head slowly and looked at him with new eyes. He wore a chambray shirt tucked into his jeans, the sleeves rolled up to his elbows. Typical farmer clothing. Somehow they didn't go with the professionally styled haircut and the expensive gold watch strapped to his wrist. He reminded her of a man selling seed corn in a television commercial—a man dressed for the part he was playing, but obviously, so obviously, not of the soil.

Suddenly everything swung into focus. "I'll be downstairs shortly, and we can discuss the sale." Her eyes burned up at him resentfully.

"What sale?"

"Don't play games with me, Mr. Lang. I may have had a blinding headache, but I know perfectly well what I said. You've won! I'll sell our share of the farm to you. But I don't intend to discuss it in the bedroom."

"Then what happened here in this bedroom last night meant nothing?"

120

She could tell he was angry, but his voice remained calm. "Right. You're stupid if you thought differently."

Rage flashed in his eyes, darkened his face, and hardened the lines of his mouth. "You're the one who's stupid if you can't forgive a human error."

"Some error! You burned down my barn, destroyed what my family and I have worked for all our lives, and you want to chalk it up to a little human error?" She snorted in disgust and raised up in bed so suddenly the pain behind her eyes rocked her. "I should have sold out to you when you first came here. Now I don't suppose you're willing to offer the same price."

"I'm not offering *any* price," he said through clenched teeth.

"I can force you!"

"How? You'll have to put up the money to buy my share before you can force me to buy yours."

Angrily Iris threw back the covers and put her feet on the floor. She still had on her jeans and sweat shirt. "You're lower than I thought!"

"I can get lower!"

"You did. Last night!"

He moved so fast she had no time to move away from him. His hands gripped her shoulders. "Damn you!" he muttered.

"Get your hands off me," she hissed.

He dropped his hands and moved away. "There's an old Chinese proverb that says, 'If you are patient in one moment of anger, you will escape a hundred days of sorrow.' I advise you to remember that."

"You know what you can do with your Chinese proverb."

"I know what I'd like to do to you—shake some sense into that stubborn head of yours!"

"Then you'd better think again!" She stood stock still, waiting for the dizziness to pass. She didn't care that her hair hung in strings, having come free from the ribbon she'd tied at the nape of her neck, or that her face was swollen. "Brenda and I will move out. *You* can run the farm and send us our share, or the profit, or whatever as I've done for you these past years."

"You and Brenda are staying right here." His voice was deadly calm. "You won't disrupt that girl's life because of your damned stubbornness." His hands on her shoulders gripped her cruelly, and he crushed her to him. "I'm mighty tempted to slap you!"

She believed him and was frightened, but determined not to show it. "And add abuse to your list of little human errors?"

"When I get my hands on you, abuse is the last thing I'm thinking of," he grated out.

She pushed at his chest. "Let me go! I don't want you to touch me ever again. I hate it!"

"You didn't hate it last night."

Shame and anger seared through her. How could he be so vile as to remind her? Instinctively, she felt he was about to kiss her, and desperately and recklessly she tried to defend herself with words. They fell from her lips in a torrent of blatant lies, out of place, wrong, uncharacteristic of her.

"Can you blame me for taking advantage of your expertise? I knew you were an experienced lover, and who better to take my virginity? I've been embarrassed because of it. Many times I'd have gone to bed with someone I cared about, but I didn't want him to know. You served my purpose very well!"

"You're a liar!" he snarled. His hands encircled her upper arms, and her eyes darkened as his fingers hardened like steel bands about her. His face was like a stone statue, hard and bitter. Iris was sure he was going to hit her. Instead his hands slipped up around her throat and his mouth came down on hers savagely, relentlessly, prying her lips apart, grinding his teeth against her mouth. His thumbs beneath her chin held her head immobile. She moaned, and struggled.

He pushed her against the edge of the bed. She fell, and he followed her down. Winded, they lay there breathing hard. His dark red hair shut out everything, and his mouth burned, delved, bruised her now, forcing her to lay still. His hands moved over her, tunneled under the sweat shirt, his fingers finding the high, warm swell of her breasts.

He lifted his head, and she gasped for breath. Her heart hammered so hard that her ears were ringing. She couldn't think. She couldn't speak. He stared at the white skin laid bare by the bunched-up sweat shirt. No bra covered her rounded breasts. He saw for the first time the rosy nipples he had caressed last night. His eyes flickered to her face, and she shook her head in silent protest.

"Be my Iris of last night, darling," he whispered. She heard the words as if mouthed by some distant mythical person. Desperately she fought down the desire to give up, surrender to the yearning building inside her.

"Nooo . . ."

"You know what happened between us was something like . . . like a miracle. To hold you like this—" His strange, thickened voice broke off; his mouth pressed against her throat, then slid up to close over her mouth. He kissed her gently now. Her mouth trembled. The searching movement of his lips parted hers, and he began a sensuous exploration of the inside of her mouth with his tongue.

The coaxing movement of his mouth awakened a strange, melting heat inside her. One of his hands moved back and forth across her breast in a soft, possessive caress. Loving the feel of the new calluses on his palm, she reacted automatically; her nipple became erect and sent messages throughout her body. Wetness sprang between her thighs. The weight of him felt so good! It took every ounce of her self-control to keep from wrapping her arms about him and flying away with him into the sensuous world where there was only his hard male strength to cling to.

"You see how it is with us." He breathed into her mouth, and his body moved urgently against hers.

Abruptly, she went cold, as though he had lifted her out of the depths of sexual chaos. "No," she said tightly. "Get off me!" She twisted out from under him, and he released her.

He sat on the edge of the bed, breathing hard, and watched her pull the sweat shirt down over her naked breasts, grab the headache pills, and head for the door. She turned.

"You've totally disrupted my life and you've destroyed the way of life I've built for Brenda. Don't you think you've done enough?" She saw him flinch as though she had struck him.

As she turned, he said quickly, "I'll admit I may have jarred you out of your humdrum existence, but I've taken nothing from Brenda. And that isn't all— I'm not going to allow you to take anything from her, either."

"I can't believe you'd attempt to control our lives! You're a stranger to us, and I despise everything about you!"

His bright blue eyes mocked her. "You're a liar, Iris," he drawled softly. "Not a word of what you've said is true, and you know it. You're hurt and miserable. I can understand that. But mouthing lies about how you hate me is juvenile, don't you think? We both know it isn't true, don't we?"

She wanted so badly to hit him that her fists curled into tight balls. Only self-respect kept her from hurling the curses that bubbled up within her. She walked down the hall, into the bathroom, and childishly slammed the door. The sound sent vibrations of pain shooting through her head.

"Why don't you slam the door, Iris?" John called from the other side.

Damn him! She looked at the door for a moment, then opened it and gave it another slam. She could hear his light laughter as he walked down the hall.

Eight

Her calm voice and placid expression masking the wrenching ache that tore at her heart, Iris managed to get through the days following the fire. Every morning she went to the fields as soon as Brenda was on the school bus. She carried with her a sandwich and a thermos of milk, and she wore her old straw hat. Driving the big green tractor, she circled the fields, pulling the disc, not knowing or caring if anything would be planted there other than a seed crop to hold the soil.

John had told her once again he would not buy her out. If it had not been for Brenda she would have offered the farm to the bank at below market value, but she couldn't do that to her sister. She hadn't approached Brenda about moving to town either, wanting to give her time to recover from one shock before adding another.

The morning the man from the farm store brought the seed corn, Iris was pushed into making a decision on a matter that had floated around in her mind since the fire.

"Mr. Lang paid for it, Miss Ouverson," the man said, and scratched his head in puzzlement.

"I see." She turned and walked to the house.

Iris spent the remainder of the morning sorting through papers in the big rolltop desk in the dining room. Years of old farm reports had been dumped there, as well as personal papers. Everything pertinent to the farm operation, including the farm-account checkbook, was put in a cardboard box. She cleaned out every scrap of paper from the desk before getting out the furniture polish. She'd never seen the desk cleaned out before. It was a comforting task to polish the wood and to clean the brass drawer pulls. When she finished she carefully rolled the top down and left the house.

When she returned to the house in the evening a man with a bulldozer was pushing the debris that had been the machine shed and the garage into a heap. Another man was scooping it up with a loader and dumping it in a truck. Iris left the tractor at the edge of the field and walked to the house.

"I've filled all the water tanks." Brenda had been rather quiet since the fire.

"That's good. I thought we'd stick a couple of frozen dinners in the oven tonight. How does that strike you?"

"We had pot pies last night." Brenda's voice held a whine that irritated Iris, but she tried not to let it show.

"Okay. How about Welsh rarebit? You like that."

"No cheese."

Glory! Where had she heard that before? Then she

remembered, and said quickly, "Then back to TV dinners."

"Are you going to fix a snack for them?" Brenda jerked her head toward the yard. "John said they'd work till they've got a place clear for a pole building. The men are coming tomorrow to put it up."

"Oh, really? That's news to me." Resentment rose in waves. "He seems to have things under control. I'm sure that includes a snack for the men."

"Oh, Iris," Brenda wailed.

"I'll get our meal started. I want you to take a box over to Mr. Lang." Iris brought the carton in from the dining room and set it on the kitchen table.

"What'll I say?"

"Nothing. He'll know what it is."

It was done. The management of the farm was in the hands of someone outside the family for the first time in its history. Iris forced her trembling legs to move around the kitchen. She prayed the lead weight in the pit of her stomach would dissolve.

Brenda came in. Iris didn't want to ask, but she did. "What did he say?"

Brenda lifted her shoulders. "Thanks." She slumped in a chair. "What's the matter with you, Iris? You've been a drag ever since the fire. Are you still mad at John? You are, aren't you?"

"Mr. Lang isn't exactly the love of my life." Heavens! Why on earth did she put it that way? A quick glance told her that the remark meant nothing to her sister. "He burned down our barn, honey. He

128

needed only to ask either of us and we'd have told him the reason there was no light in the hog house."

"He didn't mean to."

"I'm sure he didn't, but he did. Now he can manage what's left any way he wants. I've had the responsibility for five years. Let him worry about it for a while." Iris tried to keep the bitterness out of her voice. "I've been meaning to bring something up for days. Do you remember when we talked about moving to town? Would you like to do that this summer?

I'm almost sure I can get a teaching job in Central. I hear they'll need an art teacher next year."

"Move? Leave Sugar and Candy?" Misery and shock were etched in Brenda's young face.

"Alvin will board Sugar and Candy. You can come out every Saturday. In another year and a half you'll be driving the car." Please understand, honey, she pleaded silently.

"What about Buck and Boots? And Elizabeth?"

"We couldn't keep Elizabeth in an apartment, but there'd be no problem if we rented a small house." Iris opened the refrigerator. She didn't want to look at Brenda's stricken face. "I was thinking I'd sell Buck and Boots. They're getting old, and I don't ride them very much." She set her lips to keep them from trembling. "Mr. Jenson from the auction company is coming out tomorrow. There's going to be a big horse auction next Friday night." Her voice held a plea for understanding.

Iris didn't want to tell her sister that their insurance wouldn't cover the losses due to the fire and that the farm account was in the red. They would need money to live on until she got a job. They couldn't expect anything from the farm until the crops—if there were crops—were sold in the fall. She was seriously thinking about selling Grandpa's desk and a few other valuables in order to tide them over. But she couldn't have told her sister any of those things, even if she had wanted to, because Brenda burst into tears and hid her face in her folded arms.

"You don't like John! That's why you want to move away from here." She raised her head to glare at her sister.

"For heaven's sake!" Brenda had been experimenting with mascara! It was streaking down her face. The crazy thought shot through Iris's mind before she spoke. "It's a matter of economics, Brenda," she said patiently, and tried to sniff her own tears away.

"No, it isn't! John bought the seed corn and he's putting up the pole building. He said he'd loan the farm account what it needed."

"When did he say all this?"

"He talks to me lots of times. He'd talk to you, too, if you'd only—"

"Damnation! He'll own our half of the farm, too, before we know it. He isn't doing this out of the goodness of his heart!" Bitterness edged her tone and lined her face.

130

"Well, I'm not going!"

"Brenda!" Iris looked at the younger girl with amazement. For the first time in her life her little sister had defied her. "This is hard enough without having to fight you, too," she said dejectedly.

"I don't understand why you're so mean to John." Brenda stood up, her eyes flooded with tears. "If you hate him so much, what was he doing here the night the barn burned?"

It seemed to Iris that her heart fell down through her stomach to her toes. "What do you mean?"

"He was in the house at three o'clock in the morning. Everyone knows that. Iris . . ." Brenda threw her arms around her sister's waist and buried her face in her shoulder. "What do we care what anyone else thinks? If you went to bed with John, it's all right with me."

"Oh, Brenda!" If her sister had suddenly sprouted horns, Iris couldn't have been more shocked. For a long moment she couldn't move, couldn't speak. She could feel her mouth hanging slack and her knees trembling. How could she preach to Brenda about morality when she . . . "Have you been embarrassed by the talk?" she asked quietly.

"No. Some of the kids think it's neat." Her face was streaked with tears and mascara, her lashes spikey. She looked very young. "John will marry you, if you ask him."

"I wouldn't think of such a thing!" Iris's hands gripped her sister's shoulders. "And you put that thought out of your mind. Well manage. We always have."

131

"Let's stay here, Iris. Pl-eee-ze!"

"I can't make any promises, honey. You'll just have to trust me to do what I think is best for us. C'mon. Let's eat. Tell me about your day. Have you finished your math tests?"

Iris had never felt so defeated. How could things have gone so wrong in such a short span of time?

The man from the auction barn drove up the lane the next morning just as the school bus arrived. Iris cursed his timing and hoped Brenda didn't realize who he was. Her sister had said scarcely a word to her this morning and had only grunted a reply when she called out, "Have a good day."

Iris sighed and pulled her floppy straw hat down on her head. She wanted to reach Mr. Jenson before he joined the crew unloading the material for the pole building.

She was too late. He was standing beside John when she went out the door. Damn! Adding to her irritation, John walked with him to the back steps, where she stood.

" 'Morning, Mr. Jenson. Thank you for coming on such short notice."

"I want to talk to you for a moment, Iris," John said. "Will you excuse us for a moment, Mr. Jenson?"

Iris didn't look at John, but she knew from the sound of his clipped voice that he was angry.

"Sure. I'll just amble over and talk to the boys. T'was a shame about the fire, Miss Ouverson. It don't look like the same place without the barn."

"It doesn't seem like the same place, either," she said woodenly.

"What's he doing here?" John demanded as soon as the man was out of hearing distance.

"I'm not selling anything that belongs to you, if that's what you're worrying about," she snapped.

"You're not selling anything to him, period. I'm not stupid. He's a horse buyer, isn't he?"

"If you're not stupid, it's the first I've heard about it. Kindly tend to your own business."

"You are my business, you stubborn little fool!" he said tightly. His lips seemed to spit out the words. He stood with his hands in his pockets and glared at her. Abruptly he turned on his heel. "C'mon. I want to know where you think we should put the building. It'll be ten feet longer and five feet deeper than the old one." He moved away as if she were going with him. She didn't move. He stopped and spun around. "Damn you! Do you want those men to go back to town with more gossip?"

"I couldn't care less what they take back to town. I'm no more than a whore in their eyes as it is! Put your damn building wherever you want. Preferably—"

"Shut up! I'll not stand for guttersnipe talk from you! All right? I'll put the building where I think it should be, which is twenty feet back from where the old shed stood. I don't want to hear you bitching about it later. Understand?"

"I understand more than you think, Mr. Lang. I'll do

my share of the work, but when the crops are in, it's all yours. Got it?" She spat out the words in the same tone he'd used. Her head was raised so she could see him from beneath the brim of the floppy hat. Their eyes battled.

"You don't have as much horse sense in that beautiful head of yours as a . . . flea. You could learn a few things from your sister, you muleheaded little—" He seemed to catch himself just in time, and bit off the words. "I'm warning you, Iris." His finger came up under her nose, his voice more deadly because it was scarcely more than a whisper. "Don't try to take that girl away from here because you've got a hate on for me. This is her home, her security. I'll fight you every step of the way if you try it."

"You'll have to, because it'll be 'damn the torpedos and full speed ahead' when I decide what's right for us!"

"And you'll get blown right out of the water, little tug." A grin started in his eyes and spread to the rest of his face.

Iris snapped her teeth together in frustration, gave him a look that would have wilted a corn stalk, and headed for the pasture where the horses were kept. She knew she was being rude to Mr. Jenson by not calling out to him, but she was having enough trouble with the knot in her stomach and needed a few minutes alone.

Every encounter with John left her more shaken than the one before. Iris hoped the walk to the pasture would give her time to get her emotions under control. It did help. Buck and Boots came to meet her. She snapped the lead ropes to their halters, and they followed along behind her. Buck nudged her shoulder affectionately, and she had to swallow repeatedly the lumps that came up in her throat.

The horse buyer was waiting at the water tank. His experienced eyes flashed over Buck and on to Boots. He moved his hands over the black coat and gently pulled out tufts of hair.

"Shedding his winter coat," he murmured as if talking to himself. He ran his hand down the front leg and picked up the foot. "Hooves are in good shape." Boots stood obediently while the man looked in his mouth. "Nine or ten?"

"Eight. He was born here on the place."

"Ain't he the one that'll stand on the box like the Indian in the picture? *End of the Trail*, or something like that?"

"Yes, he'll do that. I've taught him several tricks." She picked up a little stick and tapped the horse on the front legs. "Kneel down, Boots. C'mon, kneel down so I can get on." The horse tossed his head, then bent his front legs and settled heavily to the ground. Iris flung her leg over his back, and he got to his feet. "Good boy." She patted his neck. "I used to ride him while standing on his rump, but I haven't done that for a long time."

"We won't have no trouble gettin' a good price for him if you'll go in the ring and show him off." He took his hat off and waved it. "Ain't neither one of 'em spooky."

"They've been handled a lot," Iris said lamely, and slid off Boots's back.

"I don't know about the other'n. He's got to be twenty if he's a day."

"He's eighteen. My dad bought him for me when he was about a year old. His mother had been killed by lightning."

"I don't know," he repeated, and ran his hands down the hind legs. Buck didn't like the touch, and laid his ears back. "Stiff in the hind quarters. I spotted that when he came in. Well, we can get somethin' for him. He's gentle. Someone may want him for a kid. Tell you what. Brush 'em up good. Get as much of that winter hair off as you can. You could even shine 'em up a little with some oil. We'll sell 'em. Ain't no doubt 'bout that." He screwed his hat down on his head. "I gotta be making tracks. Got more calls to make."

"Thank you."

"If ya ain't got no way to haul 'em, I can send the truck out and take the charge out of the sale price."

"All right. Friday morning?"

"Friday, before noon."

Iris managed to hold back the tears until the man was behind the trees and out of sight. Then she turned and put her arms around the neck of the big buckskin horse that had been hers since she was fourteen. Sobs shook her slender frame.

"I'm sorry, Buck. I'm sorry!" Her voice was a

pathetic croak. She buried her face in his dusty mane and cried as she hadn't done since she was a child.

Buck tossed his head and then stood perfectly still. Events flashed before Iris's eyes one after the other. Buck following her around the farm, more like a puppy than a horse; astride his back, racing through the fields with her thin legs clamped to his heaving sides, because she seldom took the time to put on a saddle; Buck standing quietly with his feet tangled in the barbed wire and her lying at his feet. Any other horse would have become frantic and kicked her. She would have been seriously injured or killed. She remembered now how proud she was to ride him in the Fourth of July parade, and one year had led the parade carrying the flag.

"Oh, Buck! Will you ever forgive me? What will become of you and Boots? Will some thoughtless kid run you until you're so stiff you can't walk? Will you be homesick for the pasture you've always known?" Tears streamed down her face like summer rain, and racking sobs shook her shoulders.

The horse bobbed his head and made a blowing sound with his lips, as if he understood.

Iris was so steeped in her misery that at first she didn't feel the hand on her back. When she did, she looked over her shoulder into John's face. Although her eyes were clouded with tears she could see that his were, too.

"Iris . . . sweetheart . . . don't—" He blinked rapidly. "I'm not going to let you do this." His voice quivered.

It didn't sound like his voice at all. His hand moved over her back in a comforting circular motion. Just for an instant she almost yielded to the temptation to throw herself in his arms.

It was impossible that those tears stood on his thick, stubby lashes. No, it wasn't. He was feeling sorry for her! Pity! It was more demoralizing than if he had been angry with her. She broke and ran as if the devil himself were after her.

"Iris . . ." His call floated after her, but she didn't stop until she reached the house. She caught her breath and sped up the steps to the bathroom and yanked the headache pills out of the cabinet.

After she gulped down a couple of tablets, she bathed her face and sat down on the edge of the tub. It took several minutes for her to realize that it would be easier to get herself back together if she were out in the field, where there was nothing but the tractor noise to disturb her thoughts.

She crammed the floppy hat down on her head. Then her long legs took the stairs two at a time. She sped through the dining room. In the kitchen she ran up against a wall of solid flesh and muscle. John had stepped from the side of the door to block her way. He had to fasten his hands to her shoulders to keep her from falling.

"You're getting another headache. That's two in a week."

"It isn't *your* head," she said belligerently.

"Don't go to the field today. We're not that far

behind with the work. I've got young Jerry coming to help on the weekend."

She shrugged his hands from her shoulders. "Good for you. I hope you can afford it," she said sarcastically.

"I'm going to pay his father by overhauling one of his tractor engines after the planting season."

"Good for you," she repeated, and moved to go around him, then stopped. "Didn't you learn in the Navy you're supposed to knock before entering private quarters?"

"Attack is the best defense, huh? It won't work, Iris." He moved quickly for a large man. His body blocked the doorway. "I told Jenson the horses were not for sale."

Iris gaped at him. Her mouth opened, then snapped shut. "They're not your horses!"

"If you don't want them, I'll pay you for them. What do you want?"

"Five hundred dollars each," she shouted. The price was ridiculous, and she expected to see astonishment on his face.

"Sold!"

"No!"

"The horses are not leaving this farm." He spaced each word to give them all emphasis. "You can be as stubborn and as bullheaded as you want, Iris. But I'm telling you—those horses are not leaving this farm!" He was angry, very angry, so angry that a dull red covered his face and he clenched and unclenched his hands in an effort to keep them off her. "Buck has been here all his life. I remember seeing you ride him when you were no older than Brenda. He knows every foot of that pasture. He'd die of a broken heart if he were taken to a strange place. Do you want to see him pulling a trash wagon? Or ground up for dog meat? I'd rather take my rifle out there and shoot him!"

"You wouldn't be so cruel!"

"It would be a kindness compared to what could happen to him." Under heavy, slanting brows his gaze pinned her. "What's the matter with you, for God's sake? You're making Brenda's life miserable, my life a living hell, and you're not happy with yourself. Is it because I was caught in your house when the fire broke out and the old gossips are having a field day? We can fix that. We can get married and everyone will think you're wonderful again."

His bitter, shocking words rocked her. Blood drained from her face, and her heartbeat slowed to a dull thud.

"That's very kind of you." She spoke softly. Her bitter gaze seemed glued to his face, while the tip of her tongue came out and moistened her lips. "Thank you very much, but I must decline your generous offer to save my reputation."

"Good. I don't want you pushed into marrying me for any reason except the right one."

"And that is?" Her throat was so tight the words were difficult to get out.

"Love. I'll spell it out for you. L-O-V-E. I'll marry

140

you if you love me and want to live with me, here, for the rest of your life. And because you want to share my dreams, my problems, raise my children, be my companion when we are old." His eyes raked over her and then rested on her trembling lips.

"Is that all?" she asked politely.

"No. I want you to want me every night of my life as you did the other night. I want you to give yourself to me, laugh, play, let the real Iris break through that cocoon you've built around yourself. You're as beautiful as a butterfly, but you act like an angry hornet!"

"I thank you again for the compliments. Now, as for an answer to your proposal, if it was one—it'll be a cold day in hell when I meet those qualifications. So, if you'll stand aside, I've work to do."

"Not yet. Isn't it customary to feed workers if they're here at mealtime?"

"Yes, it is. What do you plan to feed yours? I must warn you, men doing hard work have large appetites." She did her best to return his gaze coolly.

"You're not going to cooperate." The statement was soft, menacing.

"Absolutely not! Take them to a restaurant. That should put a sizeable dent in your pocketbook." She tried to slip through the door.

"Hold it!" The words were as sharp as a pistol shot and frightened her into pausing. He was beside her in an instant, and his hands closed around her upper arms. She winced at the tightness with which he held her.

"There's a limit to how far you can push me, Iris."

"There's a limit to how far you can push me, too. I've given you control of everything. You're the big *honcho* now. But I won't be your hired hand."

He yanked her to him, lowered his head, and kissed her bitterly, then pressed more hard, unloving kisses on her mouth that took her breath from her. She struggled without success and finally surrendered to his superior strength. At last he lifted his head. His arms held her so tightly she thought she would faint and her blood pounded in her temples.

"I want you in my life. I want you in my bed. And . . . hell! I want you, period!" He grabbed her hips and pulled her even tighter against the aching hardness that throbbed between them. "You've done that to me. You do it almost every time I'm with you. I'm as horny as a stallion! Dammit, I'll put up with it for a while. Then, you obstinate little cuss, you'll get yours!"

"Don't you threaten me, you . . . you woodpecker!"

He raked his scorching eyes over each feature of her face, then he laughed, a deep masculine laugh. "Iris, give up. You won't be able to hold out against me."

Her straw hat had fallen off during the attempt to avoid his kiss. She stood quietly, refusing to humiliate herself further by struggling. He held her tightly to him with an arm across her lower back while his other hand grasped the thick blond braid and brought it over her shoulder. He brushed his face with the bushy end. His eyes were full of laughter. He slid the stubby end of the braid back and forth across his lips while his eyes held hers. Then, playfully, he tickled her nose with it. She tossed her head but refused to speak.

"It's almost as much fun to tease you as it is to make love to you." He tugged on the braid, pulling her face closer, and kissed her on the nose. Pride kept her rigid. "C'mon, honey. Melt just a little and kiss me back."

Fighting the temptation to yield to the persuasive voice and gentle, coaxing lips, Iris squeezed her eyelids tightly together and tried desperately not to think about how warm and comforting it was to be held by John. She was concentrating so hard that his hand moved down her back, his long fingers delved beneath the elasticized back of her jeans and her thin panties, slid over and cupped the fullness of her rounded naked bottom, before she came out of her trance.

"What the—? Get your sneaky hand out of there!" she demanded. She pushed on his chest with all her strength. The arm across her shoulders tightened, the fingers in her jeans pinched her bottom. She let out an incredulous gasp. "Stop that!"

"Not until you kiss me." Laughter lines crinkled the corners of his eyes, and his lips were spread in a wide grin.

Helpless against his strength, Iris considered kicking him, biting him, but decided capitulation was her only recourse. Hating herself for doing it, she kissed him lightly on the lips, then moved her face as far back as his hold on her would allow.

"Un-uh! Won't do. Put your arms around my neck

and kiss me like I know you can." His voice was intimate, stirring little waves of response along her spine. His fingers caressed her flesh and traced gently down the valley between her buttocks.

Her arms moved up and around his neck, and she placed her lips on his. She heard the low triumphant sound that came from his throat, acknowledging her defeat, but she didn't care. When he lifted his lips to demand that she open her mouth, she obeyed without hesitation. With erotic symbolism, his tongue rubbed against her smooth, even teeth, and the hand in her jeans caressed her bottom. Iris felt a sudden rip in the fabric of her resentment that had so tenuously protected her from John. Swamped by mounting desire, it became impossible to remain passive. Every cell in her body surged to life, blocking out everything except the torch of his mouth that inflamed her.

A sharp rap on the door behind her brought Iris slowly out of the haze and into the present. Her mind was foggy. John raised his mouth, and she glanced over her shoulder to the woman standing on the other side of the screened door, her face a mask of shocked disapproval.

"Hello," John said, as if it were the most normal thing in the world to greet a visitor while holding her to him with one hand, the other out of sight in her jeans. "Honey, we have company." Without haste he removed his hand and tucked her shirt back into the waistband.

Stunned into silence, Iris could only stare at the visitor. Seemingly undaunted, John stepped to the door and opened it. "Come in. I'm John Lang."

Bristling with indignation, the woman swept by him and came into the kitchen. Iris felt as if she were a puppet being jerked into speaking by the pull of a string.

"Agnes Kratz," she said lamely by way of introduction.

"Stanley's mother?" John asked pleasantly, and held out his hand. Reluctantly the woman put hers into it. "You'll have to excuse me, Mrs. Kratz. I just came in to tell Iris we'll be having guests for lunch." His smile was truly charming. "There'll be three counting me, honey," he said to Iris. He lifted his hand in a gesture of farewell and went out the door.

Nine

"I never, for one minute, believed the talk going around about you and *that* man." Uninvited, Agnes sank down onto a kitchen chair as if what she'd witnessed had taken the strength out of her sturdy body.

I bet! Iris thought, and felt the hairs on her scalp leap to alert, warning her to hold onto her temper. "You should have believed it, Agnes. It's true."

"Iris! Don't be crude, dear. I've known you long enough to know you're putting up a brave front." She smoothed the cloth on the table with a patronizing gesture. "Oh, Iris, Iris, Iris. Your daddy would turn over in his grave if he could see the state this farm is in."

145

"Do you *really* think so, Agnes?"

"Yes, I do. And what's more, we've got to do something about *that* man."

Iris stood with her hands on her hips, looking at Agnes. She noted her greasy, graying hair, her pallid complexion, her narrowed eyes, her pursed lips, the righteous shake of her head.

"What do you suggest, Agnes? Poison? Shotgun? Steel trap?"

"Dear, we can pray for the Lord to deliver you out of his clutches."

Iris blinked slowly and tried not to smile. "Do you mind if we peel potatoes while we're doing it? I've hungry men to feed at noon."

"Not at all. Let me do that while you do something else. Busy hands, you know, makes talking easier."

Iris brought a sack of potatoes, a pan, and a peeler and plunked them down on the table, wishing she had the nerve to hook the chair out from under her visitor's fat bottom when she lifted and turned it to face the table. Instead she took vengeance on the round steak she took from the refrigerator and pounded it vigorously with the meat tenderizer. She floured it and put it in the electric skillet, only half listening to the drone of Agnes's voice.

"Surely you know that, dear."

"Know what?"

"Oh, I'm sorry. You couldn't hear me over the pounding. I said, he isn't good enough for a sweet girl like you."

146

"Who?" She knew who! Damned old busybody wasn't going to give up until she'd said everything she came to say.

"Old Mrs. Lang's grandson. You know his father didn't amount to anything. I can't imagine why your daddy sold to them. Me and Stanley would've been glad to buy in. Well, all is not lost, dear. This farm can be divided. Me and Stanley was looking at the plat book. The drainage ditch runs right down through the middle."

"You and Stanley have given this a lot of thought, haven't you?" Iris said pleasantly, proud of her self-control, though she was seething.

"Yes, dear. Is this enough potatoes? Now, if you're going to mash them you'll need a few more. I suggest you leave them in large pieces so they won't cook away."

"That will be fine. Thank you." Iris grabbed up the pan and dumped the peeled potatoes in the sink.

Agnes sighed. "It's so nice to be working with another woman. I've always thought of you as my own, ever since you were a little girl."

"Excuse me. I've got to get a couple of pies out of the freezer on the porch." Iris wanted to laugh and she wanted to scream, but most of all she wanted to run John Lang's body through the hay baler for getting her into this bizarre situation.

"You can't imagine what it does to me, seeing that trailer in your grove, knowing that you and that sweet child are here alone, at the mercy of that man. He's too

147

worldly for a woman like you." Agnes continued when Iris returned.

Iris slid the pies in the oven and closed the door with a bang. "And what kind of woman am I, Agnes?" she asked loudly, indignantly, responding without thinking.

"Why . . . a good woman! Whatever did you imagine I meant? You've got a college education, you're a good worker. You shouldn't waste yourself on a no-good. You owe it to yourself and your sister to stay with your own kind."

"Like you and Stanley?" Oh, God, forgive me, Iris prayed silently, but I hate Agnes so much I may be sick!

"Yes, like me and Stanley. We both love you, and we'd take that orphan child and raise her like our own."

Iris checked a gasp. "Big of you," she muttered.

"God loves even a sinful woman, dear. You need only to confess your sins."

"Let's leave the Lord out of this, Agnes," Iris said flatly. "Did Stanley send you over here to propose to me?" Her patience was wearing thin, and she was tired of playing the game. She wondered what in the world she could say that would shock the pants off this woman.

"He wants you badly." Agnes lowered her voice. "Always has."

"He wants the farm," Iris said bluntly, and reached for a stack of plates. "I've only got half a farm, with no barn or other buildings."

148

"You've got the land, dear. With Stanley's machinery it would—" Agnes broke off and fidgeted with the buttons on her smock.

And, suddenly, just the "shocker" she wanted came to mind. "It's too late," Iris said, mock sadness coloring her voice. "I couldn't expect you and Stanley to take me in and take care of me in my condition. And there's my sister, and later . . . No. All three of us can't move in on you. It's too much to ask." She heard Agnes gasping while she calmly counted out the pieces of silverware and laid them carefully on the stacked plates.

"You mean you're preg-preg-nant?"

"Agnes, do you mind if I move your purse so I can put a clean cloth on the table?" She shot a quick glance at the shocked, reddened face when she handed her the heavy bag. That's a good bit of juicy news for you to carry to the neighbors, she thought viciously. They'll love it. They already think this is the biggest little whorehouse in Iowa! Bitchiness prodded her to add a little more oil to the fire. "I appreciate your understanding, Agnes. You can be sure that I'll let everyone know that my dearest friend hasn't condemned me for my . . . ah . . . transgression. And that she'll stand by me."

Agnes shifted from one foot to the other. "Oh, dear! It's almost noon. I must be going. Stanley brought some baby chicks home. You know how I love baby chicks. I've got to see about them."

Iris smiled sweetly. "I understand. I'm sorry you have to rush off. Come back any time, Agnes."

149

As soon as Agnes was out the door, Iris giggled, suddenly feeling better. Phew, she'd really done it this time. She didn't give a damn now, but later she knew she might be sick. She listened to the car shoot off down the drive and decided she didn't need a headache pill after all.

A little later she did.

It wore on her nerves that she had been coerced into preparing the meal. Dammit! She should be outside. The day was beautiful, the air fresh and sweet-smelling. Her resentment grew. She wondered if she would ever know a carefree, happy day again, and if the time would ever come when she didn't have the feeling the world was cockeyed.

She lifted the lid on the skillet and sniffed the delicious aroma coming from the simmering steak. She heard soft footsteps and knew that John had come into the kitchen. She dropped the lid onto the pan with a clatter, swiveled to the sink, and began to break the lettuce into bite-sized chunks. Iris felt his chest press against her back, and bent at the waist to push him away from her. She knew instantly it was the wrong thing to do.

"Mmmm . . . I like that." His voice was barely a whisper in her ear. He moved closer, and his thighs rubbed against the back of her legs and hips. His arms came around her, and his hands cupped her breasts. "No bra. I like that, too!"

"Get away from me, you . . . you wart!" With all her strength she jabbed her elbow back against his midsection. His quick expulsion of breath told her the blow had landed.

"I'll get you for that," he murmured, and moved away as the back door opened.

"Something smells mighty good."

"Hello, Mr. Olson, Mr. Volk. You can clean up in the washroom. Go through the door on your right."

Iris dished up the meal, all the time aware that John's eyes were on her. She skirted around him on her trips to the table, fuming at the looks he gave her.

"Everything is ready except the salad," she said to the men when they returned from the washroom. "I've got to add the tomatoes. Go ahead and start."

"Need any help, honey?" John smiled tauntingly, knowing the endearment irritated her.

"No. But thank you for your offer, Mr. Lang." She swore she was going to kill him the minute they were alone!

Iris washed and quartered some tomatoes and placed the wedges on the beds of lettuce in individual salad bowls. A movement on the edge of the sink caught her eyes. A small green worm humped its back as it traveled along. How did you miss being washed down the drain? she asked it silently. She delivered two bowls of salad and returned for the others. The little worm was still there.

A bright little red devil with a pitchfork in its hand danced before her eyes, causing her lips to tilt at the corners. *Oh, yes! I will!* With the tip of a knife she scooped up the little worm, lifted a lettuce leaf, and dropped it in the salad bowl. And with an enormous amount of satisfaction she set the bowl beside John's plate.

The lunch conversation drifted easily into shop talk as the men discussed the merits of the different types of sheds they had erected. John carried the burden of the conversation very handily. His intelligent blue eyes honed in on each man as he spoke, making him feel as if he were drinking in his each and every word. He asked questions, recognizing their superior knowledge of their craft, and skillfully drew them out, doing more listening than talking.

They were flattered, Iris realized as she listened. They'll leave here thinking he's the greatest thing since sliced bread!

She watched as he stabbed his fork into his salad and lifted it to his mouth. Suddenly it occurred to her that the worm might crawl out of the bowl and inch its way across the table. Heaven forbid that that should happen!

The jangle of the telephone made her start visibly.

"Are you nervous today, honey?" John favored her with a grin. His hand found her knee beneath the table.

Iris ground her teeth. "Excuse me," she said tightly. She turned her back to the table when she answered the telephone.

"Hi, Iris. Mike Dalburg. How ya doin'?"

"Fine, Mike. You?"

"Doin' good. Say, would you like to go over to Brisson to the Buddy Holly Music Festival Saturday night? There'll be a couple of bands playing his music. Even some of the musicians who played in his band will be there."

"Who's going, Mike?"

"There'll be a party from the school. Donaldson and his wife will be there. They're back together, you know."

"I'm glad to hear it."

"Well . . . wha'd'ya say?"

The silence at the table behind her goaded her to reply, "It sounds like fun, Mike. What time?"

"How about eight o'clock?" he asked on a lilting note.

"Eight o'clock is fine. See you then. 'Bye."

Iris hung up the phone and swiveled. In her peripheral vision she saw John's face turned toward her. She couldn't have kept her eyes from going to his if her life had depended on it. Her mouth went dry as their eyes locked. The censorious look he leveled at her was ripe with anger. In spite of the steeliness of his gaze she allowed hers to look slightly amused, and sat down at the table once again.

"Who was on the phone?" he asked bluntly.

"A friend of mine, the Science teacher at the high school." She cursed him silently—*Oh, damn you, damn you! I'd never have said I'd go out with that Lothario if it hadn't of been for you!* Aloud she asked brightly, "Is everyone ready for pie?"

Iris stood up and began to remove the plates. Mr. Olson set his salad bowl on his plate and handed it to

153

her. John did the same. She didn't dare look in the bowl immediately, but she did peek into it on the way to the sink. There wasn't even a piece of a lettuce leaf for a worm to hide under. Ah-ha, she thought happily.

It was hard to keep the smirk off her face when she returned to the table. She picked up the bowl with her own half-eaten salad—and sucked in her breath sharply. Humping its small body along the edge of a tomato wedge was the little green worm. Clenching her jaws together and forcing her lids to shutter her eyes, she turned from the table, only to be halted by John's softly spoken words.

"Sit down and eat your salad. We can wait for the pie."

Her eyes flew to his face. She felt the red coming up in hers and fought it down with all the self-control she could command on such short notice. His pointed smile told her that he *knew!*

Iris dished up the pie and served it, but she didn't return to the table. The conversation switched to the grain embargo, and the room was awash with voices. She seriously considered leaving the kitchen—going out to the field, to her bedroom, or locking herself in the bathroom. Instead she filled the sink with soapy water and began the cleanup.

The men continued to chat about the weather, crops, farm subsidies. As her morale deteriorated further, Iris began to think anew of escape. However, before she could formulate a plan, it was too late. Chairs were being pushed away from the table. The men joshed

154

about being so full they needed a nap before they could go back to work. Individually they thanked her for the meal and left. It was too much to hope John would go with them . . . and he didn't.

"It was a good meal." He flashed her a devastating grin as he leaned against the counter. "Especially the salad."

"Thank you," she said with a formal politeness that didn't quite come off.

"You do everything well." He moved a step closer. "But . . . you're sneaky."

"Aren't we all?"

"Sweetheart, I've picked cockroaches out of a sandwich in Manila, ants out of pudding in Africa, grasshoppers out of stew in Brazil. It was no chore at all to spot that worm in my salad."

"Interesting. You can tell me your heartrending experiences another time."

"At first I thought it was an accident, but your face gave you away. You'd make a lousy poker player." A step, a turn, and he was behind her. Arms on each side of her, his body pinned her to the counter. Her head came up with a jerk. He was laughing softly. She could feel it vibrate in his chest, pressed to her back. The sound increased, then rumbled out of him until it was a deep, honest belly laugh he couldn't seem to control.

Iris stiffened her body and tried to lift her arms to push him away, but his had locked around her, and she was helpless.

"That's two things you've got to pay for," he whispered. "One for the jab in the gut before lunch and one for the worm." He nuzzled the back of her neck under her braid. The tip of his tongue explored the velvet-smooth skin behind her ear. "I always collect," he threatened softly. His hands cupped her breasts, his thumbs stroked her nipples.

Iris seethed in righteous anger, knowing she was in a classic no-win situation. Nevertheless, she had to try.

"Get your hands off me, you woodpecker, or I'll scream!"

"Oh, sweetheart! Life with you will never be dull!" He was laughing again. "You're a lot of things, but boring isn't one of them." With a quick kiss on the side of her face he walked away, still chuckling.

Completely unnerved, her heart pounding with a mixture of frustration and desire, she heard the door slam and Arthur bark a joyous greeting. She directed her anger toward the dog.

"You worthless hound. You don't have a drop of loyal blood in your body!"

It was dusk when Iris drove the tractor to the edge of the field and parked it. She sat for a long moment, her arms folded over the wheel, and looked at the new profile of the homestead. The pole building, with its yawning open front, was finished, and John was stacking the leftover building materials. Begrudgingly, she admitted he had placed it in a more desir-

156

able location than the old shed had been. Not that she'd ever tell him so, she fumed silently, and climbed down off the machine. She walked quickly toward the house, vowing she wouldn't stop even if he did call out to her.

Iris had spent the afternoon deep in thought, trying to put her priorities in order. The one thing that was uppermost in her mind was Brenda's welfare. The next few years would be important, formative years in her sister's life. She must have the security of a stable home. This would help her through the tempestuous time of change from child to womanhood. Iris had come to the conclusion that she couldn't jeopardize the things Brenda needed because she was so deeply unhappy herself. They would stay here in the farmhouse, but as soon as the crops were in she was going to make finding a job her number-two priority.

Arthur ran to meet her when she came into the kitchen. He stiffened his legs and slid across the tile floor, crashing into a chair. After he righted himself, he barked a greeting.

"Oh, Arthur," Iris said tiredly. "You are absolutely the hairiest dog in the world. Brenda!"

"Hi. I've got supper ready." Brenda was in a good mood. She had smiles all over her face.

"Honey, you haven't brushed Arthur. Hair is coming off him in patches. If we had a spinning wheel we could go into the dog-yarn business."

"I'll brush him tomorrow. I promise." Brenda

launched herself at her sister like a missile. "John said you're not going to sell Buck and Boots. He said there was money in the bank for us to draw on until the crops were sold." She wrapped her arms around Iris's waist and tried to lift her off the floor. "When I saw the sale-barn truck drive in this morning I almost got off the bus. I worried all day! I love you, Iris, sister, jailer, and slave driver. When I get out of school I'm going to work and take care of you. 'Course . . . you could marry John, and I wouldn't have to." She ended on a hopeful note.

"I love you, too, honey." Iris hugged her, ignoring the last remark. "I don't know what I'd do without you. I want you to have the very best education we can get for you, which means, exuberant miss, you've got to keep those grades up so we can apply for a scholarship."

"I will, Iris. I'd do anything for you."

"Oh? . . ." Iris drew back and grinned at her. "How about cleaning the bathroom after supper?"

"Bathroom? Aw, Iris . . . I've got homework."

Iris laughed aloud for the first time that day. Brenda had a way of putting things on an even keel.

Brenda lay on the bed with a pained look on her face. "What'er'ya goin' out with ol' Dalburg for? All he wants is sex!"

The look Iris gave her was a mixture of frustration and surprise. "How do you know that, Miss Know-it-all?"

"He's always hugging up to ol' lady Hanley when he thinks no one's looking. Ardith saw him put his hand on her bottom."

"Ardith's good at stretching things. You told me that yourself." Iris tch-tch'ed at her sister and began flipping through the hangers in her closet. "What do you think of this?" She pulled out a fuchsia-red dress. She liked the color, but not the neckline, a shallow vee in both front and back.

"It's too bright. You'd look like a streetwalker." Brenda watched her sister slap the hook back on the rod with more force than necessary. "I'm not blind, you know. I watch *Vice Squad,* and all that."

"I'm not blind, either, sweetie. Get your feet off my bedspread." Iris was looking at a terra cotta cotton dress with a high neck and full sleeves.

"I like that."

Iris hung it back. "What are you trying to do? Sabotage my date?"

"You're going to need all the help you can get," Brenda advised. "You said when you went out with him before he had more hands than a centipede had legs."

"Maybe you're right." Iris took the dress out again and hung it on the hook on the door. She wasn't looking forward to the date. She'd had a set-to with Brenda, who'd wanted to stay at home alone. Her argument was that John would be nearby. It was finally settled when Iris called Jane Watts and asked if Brenda could spend the night. It was a trade-off. Stacy had spent several weekends at the farm while Jane accompanied her husband on business trips.

Iris lay back in the tub of warm suds and hoped the evening would go fast. She'd castigated herself time and again for agreeing to go. Brenda was more right about Mike than she realized. And Iris wasn't looking forward to his suggestive remarks and his dirty jokes.

Dreamily, she wondered how it would feel to be dressing to go out with a man you really cared about. Strange, she thought. I've been to bed with John, but I haven't been out to dinner with him, or to a show. It was still hard for her to believe the intimacy they'd shared. Now it seemed to her it was something she had dreamed, a very pleasant, wonderful dream— seeking male hands caressing her. Hard, warm naked flesh against hers, husky whispers, followed by seeking lips . . .

Ten

Iris was glad Mike Dalburg had a talent for small talk even though his remarks were almost always preceded by the words *I, I'm,* or *I've*. It made the thirty-mile drive to Brisson endurable, if not enjoyable. All she had to do was add an occasional "oh, really" or "how nice." It was enough to keep him going. He had made his move as soon as Brenda got out of the car in front of her friend's house. Mike had put his hand on her thigh to keep her from moving over. He was the kind of man who would have loved to have the reputation

160

of a superstud. Iris had firmly removed his hand, slid across the seat, and huddled next to the door.

It was all John's fault that she was out with this aging Don Juan. No, she had to admit, it wasn't anyone's fault but her own. She'd been so rattled by John that she'd actually thought she was getting back at him by accepting this date with Mike.

Mike parked the car and turned in the seat to smile at her. His perfectly capped teeth looked as if they could be used in a commercial. *Drop a tablet in a glass of water, folks, and soak your teeth until the water clears.* He was combing more hair forward now to cover his receding hairline. She wondered what he used on his moustache to make it so startlingly black. Was it hair dye, eyebrow pencil, or mascara? She hid a giggle behind a cough, then smiled at him. It wasn't his fault that for the rest of her life she would compare every man she met with a tall, broad shouldered, blue-eyed, redheaded woodpecker, who could hypnotize her with his wide, cheek-slashing grin.

Nostalgia gripped Iris when they entered the dim ballroom. Couples were dancing to *Peggy Sue*. It brought back memories of other times she had been here, hundreds of years ago, it seemed, before responsibility for her sister and the farm had sapped her youth. She let Mike guide her to a crescent-shaped booth where Jim Donaldson and his wife, recently reunited, were sitting.

"Hello, Carol, Jim." She slid into the booth and accepted their warm smiles of welcome.

"I hope this booth is large enough. Several more couples from the school are joining us." Jim seemed happy, years younger.

Mike got the waiter's attention. "What'll you have, pretty lady?"

Iris seldom drank, but she felt the need of something to help her get through the evening. "Rum and coke, please."

Their drinks arrived, followed closely by Syble Brinkman, the music teacher, and her husband. They immediately engaged Jim and Carol in conversation, leaving Iris to suffer Mike's whispered flattery. When he suggested they dance she accepted with relief.

There were a lot of things about Mike she didn't like, but his dancing wasn't one of them. He was good. He moved around the floor like a professional, being careful to allow Iris time to get warmed up before he tried a series of difficult steps. He wanted to look good, so his partner must look good. And Mike concentrated so hard on his dancing that he had no time for insincere flattery or roaming hands. They danced to several numbers, and when they left the floor they went by the bar so Mike could get another drink.

The two couples were still in the booth, and the talk centered around whether or not the school superintendent was going to retire. Iris sat quietly and listened to the music. There wasn't anything she could have added to the conversation if she had wanted to.

The lights in the ballroom dimmed even more, and

the band swung into a medley of old favorites—
That'll Be The Day, Donna, Chantilly Lace. It was
almost as if she'd been transported back into the days
of saddle shoes and full skirts over layers of net
cancan slips.

"Hello, everyone."

The lilting voice jarred Iris back to the present. She
looked up and sucked in her breath, dismayed to see a
beaming Louise Hanley at the end of the booth.
Behind her, dwarfing her, was John. He looked hard at
Iris. There was most definitely a storm warning in the
blue depths of his eyes. She was startled. What did it
mean? Was he angry to find her included in the party?
Tough! Her lips curled upward, and she gave him the
benefit of her best haughty expression.

Introductions were made all around. The talk
resumed, with Louise taking the lead, laughing and
gesturing, clearly delighted to be with John.

This had to be the most miserable night of Iris's life,
she thought wretchedly. Would it ever end? Mike's
hand covered hers, where it lay on the table, and she
asked, "Why are we wasting this good music?"

Pleased, Mike smiled smugly and asked Louise and
John to excuse them. John stood. Louise, blatantly
eager for John's attention, hung on his arm, looking up
at him adoringly. Iris threw her a disgusted look
before her eyes slid to John's. She felt a quick flash of
embarrassment. He'd read her thoughts. She saw just
a flicker of an eyelid. Had he winked at her?

"C'mon, small stuff," he said in a low drawl to

Louise, "we may as well dance, too, as long as we're on our feet."

"I haven't finished my drink." Louise pouted and melted against him. The top of her head came even with his shoulder.

Iris moved with Mike onto the dance floor. She couldn't keep her eyes from following the other couple. They look like Mutt and Jeff from the funny papers, she thought irritably. She hoped John would step all over her size 3A shoes and Louise would throw up on his XL sport coat.

Mike pulled her tightly against him, and she followed his lead. "My favorite music, my favorite girl." He held her away from him so he could see her face. There was scarcely an inch difference in their heights. "So it isn't true after all?"

"Is that why you asked me out?" Her smoky eyes blazed into his. She made no pretense of not knowing what he referred to.

He laughed softly and whirled her around. "You know better than that. I've always had a *thing* for you."

"I know. The same *thing* you've had for every other woman in town," she said coolly.

"I love it when you're like this!" His hand slipped down to her hip.

"Regardless of what you've heard, Mike, I've no more intention of sleeping with you now than I did when you took me out before. So move your hand off my rear or I'll slap you!"

"Hey, baby. Don't get so steamed up." His hand slid back to her waist, and they danced in silence.

Now and then, Iris caught a glimpse of a dark red head and broad shoulders. Louise was snuggled against his chest. She didn't want to think the raging pain that knifed her heart was jealousy. She'd always felt jealousy was a wasted emotion. But there it was, eating at her, and there was nothing she could do but endure it.

The music stopped. Mike seemed subdued. They passed the bar, and he bought another drink. Iris hadn't realized he was such a heavy drinker. He was holding it well, she thought, but if he had any more she knew who would be driving home. As they neared the booth, Mike's arm went across her shoulders. She let it remain there only because she saw John watching them.

Louise was seated. John was paying the waiter. He'd ordered more drinks, including another for Mike. Iris shook her head, feeling sick, when she saw Mike gulp the drink.

"Might as well dance with my partner," John said casually, and grabbed her hand. "Excuse us, folks."

"But, John, your drink will get warm." Louise used her girlish voice, but her eyes were hard when they rested on Iris.

"Mike can drink it. I'll get another when we come back."

Iris started to protest, but he hooked her close to his side and she went along, knowing perfectly well he was capable of creating a scene. *Might as well dance with my partner!* The words almost scalded her. Heat seemed to drain from her trembling body down to her toes, leaving her cold, wooden.

Shielding her with his large frame from the stares of those in the booth, his arms encircled her and pulled her so close to him that the buttons on his coat hurt her breast. When he began to move it was impossible not to follow his lead. He lifted his arm, pushing hers up. It went around his shoulders. Her hand came to rest at the base of his neck, her fingers curled into the thick hair at his collar.

"Aw . . . this is more like it." His murmur was a moist tickling in her ear. "I hate dancing with short women."

"You should have thought of that before you asked her out." Cool words came out of a hot, tight throat.

"I had no choice," he whispered, his chin worrying her cheekbone.

"Oh? I suppose someone was standing over you with a whip," she snapped.

"You forced me to ask her out. It's your fault. What made you accept a date with that dandy? Did you do it to spite me?"

"Don't flatter yourself," she said, much too fast. "And he isn't a dandy."

"Damn near it. A drunk, too, if I'm not mistaken." He chuckled when she refused to argue. "Are you still mad because Stanley's mother caught us with my hands in your pants?"

"Don't be crude." She tried to draw away from him, but his arms tightened. He laughed, and she could feel it all up and down her body. "I suppose you think it's funny that my reputation is in shreds," she managed to say coolly.

"I may be forced to make an honest woman out of you yet." His fingers moved up her back and around to stroke the side of her breast. "Now, don't sputter. Be quiet. I want to enjoy this. It'll be over all too soon." He pressed his lips to her ear, and she felt a small tug when he pulled at her earring with his lips. "Mmmm . . . sexy woman. You smell so good."

His feather-light kisses along the sensitive skin in front of her ear were sending the familiar butterfly wings to her stomach. "Don't do that! People are looking. We're not exactly an inconspicuous couple, you know."

"I know. You're the most beautiful woman here. I like you in this soft stuff." His hand moved the material of her dress caressingly over her back. "A movie star doesn't hold a candle to you, Farmer Brown." He chuckled again. She knew he could feel the pounding of her heart. "You're wearing a bra tonight. Good."

What did he mean by that? Iris didn't want to wonder about the *why's* or *wherefore's*. She gave herself up to his tight embrace and simply enjoyed it. Her heart throbbed in her throat, and she couldn't move her cheek from his. Her eyes were half closed and filled with a look of intense longing. For the briefest moment she forgot anyone else existed except the two

167

of them. She nestled her cheek closer against his and moved her arm further around his neck.

"Mmmm . . . you're very soft and sweet tonight, my wild Iris rose," he whispered.

"With that blatherin' tongue 'tis sure you've kissed the Blarney stone, me boy," she whispered back.

His laugh was low and private and sensuous. He lowered his head slightly and blew down her neck. "That isn't what I want to do, but it'll have to do for now."

Iris floated in a golden haze, aware only of the lean, strong body pressed to hers, the warm hands holding her, the intimate touch of their moving thighs. He moved his face, and she tilted her head slightly to look at him. Emotion was there. But what emotion? Was it love? Caring? Whatever it was, it had the power to stop her breath. His arms tightened convulsively when her lashes fluttered down. Wordlessly he pressed his cheek to hers again, and she surrendered all control to him. They glided around the room to the strains of a slow waltz. Iris felt enchanted.

John brought them to a halt when the music stopped, and he took a step back from her, letting his hands rest on her hips. He looked at her for a long moment and then lifted a hand to finger-comb the hair back from her temple.

"I like your hair done up like that. You look cool and confident like a princess." A slow smile lit his face. "I'm sure Old MacDonald didn't have anything like you down on his farm."

"I'll bet he didn't have a sailor, either," she said softly. There was a slight tremor when she spoke, but her smoky eyes held his unwaveringly.

"I can believe that." His laugh was deep, and people turned to look at them.

His hand rested on her waist as they walked back to the booth. It didn't go unnoticed by Louise, who sat alone with Mike. She stood so Iris could move in beside him.

"Thanks for bringing him back," she said brightly, as if Iris had led John to her on a leash.

"He's all yours." She wished her voice had been stronger.

"I know." Louise glanced at her over her shoulder, then looked up into John's face. "Shall we dance? I think Mike wants to he alone with his date."

Iris would have loved to wring her neck.

"Sure." John stood stock still for a moment, but Iris refused to look up at him. "Don't go away, you two," he said, and with his hand on Louise's back urged her toward the dance floor.

"Why didn't you come with *him?*" Mike's words were slurred, and Iris heard a warning bell ring in her ears.

"He didn't ask me," she snapped.

"He's playing you and little twitchy-fanny against each other. Smart of him."

Mike was drunk, very drunk. An angry flush heated Iris's cheeks. "I think we'd better go."

"Why? Because *he* won't be coming back for a

while? He won't, you know. *She'll* see to it."

"You're disgusting!" Iris moved along the smooth seat and stood. Her haughty expression intimidated him enough that he got to his feet and lurched after her when she headed toward the door.

Iris threaded her way between the tables and booths, not knowing or caring if he was following. At the entrance she turned and waited for him. He had bumped into a couple and was trying to apologize. He gestured toward Iris, and they turned to look at her. She found her temper rising.

"Give me the keys, Mike."

"Nooooo one's driving my car but me."

"Give me the keys. Or as soon as you get in the car I'll call the police and have you arrested for drunk driving. You're in no condition to get behind the wheel." She looked at him steadily.

"You're a . . . bitch. That's what you . . . are. I should'a stuck with li'l ol' twitchy-fanny."

"Iris—" She heard John's voice before she looked over her shoulder and saw him. His long legs were eating up the distance between them. Louise was doing her best to keep up. "You're not leaving with him!"

She stared at him, observing almost impersonally the muscles that bunched along his jaw. "I don't care to stand here and make a spectacle of myself arguing. I'm leaving, either with or without him. But I'll drive him home if he'll give me the car keys."

"I'll take you home."

"I came with him, and I'll leave with him, if possible." Her temper was rising again. Louise clinging to John's arm reminded her of a monkey clinging to a vine.

"Give her the keys," he said to Mike in the commanding voice he must have used on young recruits. When Mike hesitated, he said, "Give them to her or I'll throw you down and take them."

"Aw-right. Ya don't have to get . . . nasty." He dug into his pocket and brought the keys out dangling from one finger, grinning foolishly.

John snatched the keys from his hand and handed them to Iris. "I'll follow you back to town. Take him home and I'll pick you up."

"John!" Louise protested. "They'll be all right. Let's not go yet. The place is just beginning to liven up."

"Stay, by all means, and enjoy yourselves. Don't cut your evening short because of Mike and me." Iris turned and went through the double doors.

Relieved to be out in the cool night air, she walked quickly to the car and slid behind the wheel. Mike got in on the passenger side and slammed the door.

"You sure turned out to be a . . . dud," he muttered.

Iris almost smiled at his childish pushing. He wanted to quarrel with her, but she remained silent and drove the car out of the parking lot and onto the highway. Headlights flashed in the rearview mirror. At the first stop sign she glanced in the side mirror and saw John's station wagon behind them. She didn't know whether she was glad he cared enough to follow her to see that she got safely back to town or whether she was irritated that he thought she was unable to handle things herself.

Mike slumped down in the seat. Phew! The smell of his breath was enough to make her sick. She rolled down the window so the cold wind could fan her face. She drove automatically, trying not to think of Louise snuggled up to John's side in the car behind.

By the time she pulled the car to the curb and parked it in front of Mike's apartment building, he was snoring. She would have left him sitting there, but John opened the door and, after a brief, disgusted glance, hauled him out and stood him up beside the car.

"Which apartment is his?"

"How should I know? Ask Louise." The snippy remark slipped out, and she instantly regretted it. She put the car keys in Mike's coat pocket.

"We can't leave him out here. Go open the door."

Iris couldn't tell whether John was angry or not. She could see Louise sitting in the middle of the seat, watching, gloating. John stooped, let Mike fall over his shoulder, and hoisted him up. Iris opened the glass-paned door of the apartment building, and John angled his body and Mike's through. He stopped and scanned the names over the mailboxes.

"Wait for me here," he barked at her.

Iris stood beside the door, hating to have to go out to the car and be driven home like some errant teenager whose date had gone sour. She watched John carry

Mike up the stairs. He seemed to do it so effortlessly—the same way he'd carried her. Stop it, Iris! Don't think about that night. Better straighten yourself out, my girl, before you go out to face Miss "twitchy-fanny." She stifled a giggle. Where had Mike picked up such a phrase?

When John came back down the stairs, she was once more on the defensive, and when he took her arm to walk her to the car, she firmly removed it from his grasp.

There was plenty of room for her on the seat without crowding the door. Louise sat snugly against John. Even her knees were tucked beneath his long thigh.

"What in the world did you do to Mike, Iris? I've never seen him like that."

"I didn't do anything to him," she said with exaggerated patience. "He drank like he was going to be hung within the hour."

"He likes you a lot, and was looking forward to this date. He's really a nice guy. He said the two of you had great times together."

Iris was well aware Louise was trying to convince John that there was a relationship between her and Mike. "I've only had one other date with him, Louise. Believe me, it wasn't all that great."

Louise lapsed into silence. Iris had expected her to pant and purr all the way to the farm. Suddenly, she was aware of the reason for the silence. John was taking her home. When they turned down the darkened street, Iris could almost feel the hostility radiate from Louise, who took her hand from his leg. Iris almost felt sorry for her . . . almost, but not quite.

John got out of the car and held the door open for Louise to slide under the wheel. She didn't answer when Iris said, "Good night."

Okay, so she'd made another enemy. Iris sank down in the seat and wondered for the hundredth time about the kick in the teeth fate had given her at this time in her life. She kept her face turned firmly away from Louise's door.

John was chuckling that deep, amused chuckle that so irritated her, when he got into the car. "What's so funny?"

"Louise. She's mad as a hornet." John drove away from the curb, and his left hand groped for her. "Come over beside me. We've finally got rid of those two." His hand found her arm, and she had no choice but to move to the middle of the seat.

"She has a right to be mad. You should've taken me home first. She was your date."

"Only because I couldn't have you. This could have been avoided if you'd have mentioned you wanted to go to the dance. As it is, I had to scramble around to find a date when . . ."

"When you wormed it out of Brenda."

"Yeah. She's a fun kid. I haven't been around a girl her age before." His hand reached down to caress her knee. "Do you want something to eat? We can stop at the restaurant on the highway."

"No," she said quickly. Then she modified it. "No,

but thanks." She grasped his wrist and gently but firmly removed his hand from her knee. Not because she didn't enjoy his touch, but because she was trembling and didn't want him to know it. She was tired, sick at heart. The emotional strain of the last few weeks as well as hard work had sapped her strength, and it wouldn't take much to push her over the brink.

What seemed like endless minutes later John pulled the station wagon into the carport and turned off the lights. Iris reached for the door handle and pressed it, but it was locked. He turned in the seat to look at her.

"You're working too hard."

Surprised by his words, she turned and found him closer to her. She tried for lightness in her voice. "No harder than you have. All farmers put in long hours during the planting season."

"The season is over. I want you to spend more time at the house." It was the last thing she had expected him to say, and his voice held a tenderness that was her undoing.

"I have to put in the garden." She turned her head away and tried the door handle again. She took a deep, steadying breath. "Thanks for the ride."

John reached out to cradle the nape of her neck and pull her toward him. Iris felt the strength drain out of her.

"Don't. Please . . . don't," she said feebly. Control left her, and mortification set in when she burst into tears. "I'm . . . I'm . . . sorry!" She was crying in great, ragged gulps, and tried to put her hands over her face, but her arms were pinned to her sides as his arms went around her.

"Darling, what's the matter?" His voice was husky, pleading. "Are you sick? Is it one of your headaches? Don't cry. I can't stand to see you like this." His words were interspersed with quick, light kisses on her wet face. "Tell me. Tell me what's wrong. Have I goaded you too far?"

"It isn't your fault." She struggled to gain control. "I haven't managed my life very well. I can see that now. I'm naive, self-centered where the farm and Brenda are concerned. I've let them become my whole life. I've tried to be the captain of my own soul and behave well whatever happens, but I've made a mess of it."

He cuddled her in his arms, and his lips moved over her face, avoiding her mouth so she could talk. "I've blamed you for everything, when the truth is I don't know how much longer I could have gone on alone. I know you didn't mean to burn down the barn. . . . And you'll probably do a better job with the books than I could have done. I don't like myself anymore."

"Shhh . . . I thought you felt guilty about being with me . . . that night."

"No. I wanted you to make love to me." *What I really wanted was for you to love me,* she cried silently.

"You've been lonely, sweetheart. You've had so much responsibility, and I came along with my trailer and really threw a spanner in the works here at the farm." He tried to kiss the wetness from her eyes. "I pushed too hard, sweetheart, when I really wanted to grow on you gradually. I'm told that's the basis for a lasting relationship. I made a wave and hit it head on, because I was so glad I'd found you. I care about you, darling. I care very much." He folded her closer to him and lifted her arm to encircle his neck. "I want to build my life around you and Brenda. I was hoping you'd come to care for me." He buried his face in her hair. "I hadn't planned to tell you this until I thought there was a chance for me."

"John . . ." she whispered shakily. She was unable to believe what he was saying.

"We can make it work, darling," he told her huskily.

Iris smiled through her tears. "Are you saying that you . . . care for me?"

"I'm saying I love you." His voice shook, and his arms held her so tight the air exploded from her lungs.

When his mouth closed over hers, Iris quit smiling, but inside her, laughter spread out. The kiss was long and sweet, and conveyed a message too poignant for mere words. It was slow and deep and warmed her, joining both their mouths in sweet excitement. She could feel the steady beat of his heart and the quickening of her own.

"I love you, love you, love you!" He said it against her mouth, her ear, her nose.

"And I love you," she cried happily. She had to touch him, was frantic to touch him. Her hand found its way to his waist and the belted trousers, then lower to the straining zipper.

She felt the breath expelled harshly from his lungs, and could almost feel the blood surge through his body. She moved her hand from the outline of his tumescence.

"I'm sorry," she gasped when his mouth left hers.

"Sorry? I don't want to hear that word for the next . . . forty years!"

Before the wildfire of emotion could sweep them into another burning kiss, Iris drew back until the tip of her nose rested against his and said in a sexy stage whisper, "Your place or mine?"

Happiness bubbled up, and laughter broke from their lips and gleamed in their eyes.

Eleven

It was one of those rare nights when bodies spoke silently, ignited, and burned on for hours. It was almost dawn when he whispered to her, "Go to sleep, darling. I want to hold you in my arms while we sleep."

Almost immediately, Iris fell into a deep, satisfying slumber, but she was still subconsciously aware of the warm male body pressed spoon fashion to her own, the heavy weight of the arm across her body, and the hand that cupped her breast. It was a wonderful way to sleep. It was even more wonderful to wake in her lover's arms.

Something tugged on her earlobe. She shook her head, but the pull persisted. Then warm air was blown into her ear. She turned her head, and her nose collided with another nose, and lips nipped at hers. She was lying on her back, John on his side watching her. Her legs were looped over muscular thighs that were drawn up tightly to her bottom. A large hand spanned her stomach, and fingers dipped and squeezed.

" 'Mornin'," he whispered just before his mouth covered hers.

" 'Mornin'," she whispered the instant she was able. "What time is it?"

"Time to make love again." His hand moved up to her breast and his palm circled slowly.

"The chores . . . "

"All done. Farmer Brown was up while Mrs. Brown was sleeping. He wanted this waking time with his lady."

"I wonder why." She circled his neck with her arms and rubbed his nose with hers.

"Want me to jog your memory?"

"Uh-huh."

He gently spread the thighs looped over his and she felt a prodding against the part of her that throbbed with heat and moisture.

She gasped. "You're indecent!"

"Yeah. But wait till I get the mirror put on the ceiling," he threatened huskily, and covered her mouth with his before she could protest. They kissed deeply, as lovers long familiar with each other. "You taste soooo good. You're sweet, sexy, and I'm smitten. I've been all over the world and I found this in Iowa.

Unbelievable!" He muttered all those words as if talking to himself.

Later her yawn turned into a smile, and she stretched out on the comfortable bed. He peeled down the sheet and stooped to kiss her breast. "Wanton woman," he said intensely, and gave her a lecherous smile. "Get out of bed and fix my breakfast."

She laughed joyously. "Like this?"

"If you're going to fry bacon—no. If you're going to poach eggs—yes." He pulled on her nipple with his lips. "On second thought, I'll have my breakfast right here."

"Don't start anything you can't finish, sailor," she said with the confidence of a secure lover. She laughed with pure happiness. She would never have dreamed she would say such a thing.

"Is that a challenge?" he growled.

"No, no!" His hand found her ribs and raked them playfully. They rolled on the bed, wrestled, tangled in the bedclothes.

"Then, heave-ho, me beauty!" He tossed her out of bed and swiftly sprang up when she landed on her feet. He caught her close to him. They stood in an ardent embrace, naked bodies straining together from knees to lips. "Look." He turned her slightly so she could see them in the full-length mirror that covered the closet door. "Don't we fit well together?" His voice was low, husky, and she could feel his desire stirring against her softness.

"You're right . . . for once," she teased, and wound

180

her arms around him and her hair about his neck. Breakfast was forgotten.

They showered together in the minute stall after John pinned her hair on the top of her head and found a plastic sack to cover it. They stood under the warm spray, kissing, touching, laughing, until the hot water was used up and they couldn't stand the cold water that came directly from the deep well. Then, wrapped in one of John's bathrobes, Iris ran across the yard to the farmhouse when John, from a lookout on his porch, gave the all-clear signal.

Jane Watts called later to say Brenda had gone to early church services with her family, and they were taking her along to dinner with them. She would be home by one o'clock. It would be a long time before Iris forgot that time. Not because it was the time when Brenda came home—she arrived a few minutes earlier—but because of what happened afterwards.

Brenda came bouncing into the house saying she wanted to change into jeans so she could ride Sugar. Iris smiled happily, knowing how pleased her sister would be when she heard the news. She and John had agreed to tell her together.

In a happy daze, Iris was only mildly curious when the long white convertible with a woman behind the wheel drove up the farm lane and stopped at the door. Thinking she was lost and seeking directions, Iris went to the back door and onto the step. The woman sat looking at her, her arm resting on the top of the door. Her hair was even lighter than Iris's, and was held back with a pale blue silk scarf that matched the sweater she wore. Iris, in her jeans and knit shirt, her thick braid hanging down her back, her face free of makeup, felt unattractive, even hickish, in comparison.

Something about the woman and the quiet way she watched her approach slowed her feet and caused a heavy plop of fear to drop on her heart. Suddenly she knew who she was, and panic squeezed her throat.

"Hello, Iris." The woman raised thin-plucked brows. "You never change. But I must say the old place has a new look. I see you've had a fire. Too bad it didn't take that ancient wreck of a house."

"What are you doing here?"

"I'll give you three guesses. You were always rather dense and dull, Iris. I see you haven't grown out of it, although . . . Good heavens! You must be past thirty. You were just a couple of years younger than I was when I married your father. Why wasn't I notified when he died?"

"There was no reason to notify you. You're not a member of our family." All the old hatred and resentment of this woman boiled up in Iris.

"I've learned that the custody of my daughter was transferred to you. I want to see her. I want to spend some time with her. I want us to get to know each other."

I want . . . I want. She was still the same. More beautiful, more confident, but still selfish and demanding.

Protective instincts rose in Iris. She wouldn't allow this woman to spoil Brenda's life. She had John to stand beside her now. She no longer had to face this alone.

"I-r-is! Where's Candy's halter? It was here on the porch yesterday."

When Brenda stuck her head out the door, Monica got out of the car. She was tall, extremely thin, and dressed in expensively cut white slacks and slender-heeled shoes. A large diamond glittered on her finger when she fluttered her hand in Brenda's direction. Brenda came out and stood on the step, curious, and puzzled more by her sister's rigid, defensive stance than by the beautiful woman.

"Brenda, dear. Do you remember me? You're almost as tall as I am. Oh, for heaven's sake! I can't believe it." She laughed a tinkling, careful laugh. Brenda's brows drew together, and she glanced at Iris. "I'm Monica, your mother." Monica laughed again. "I've had my hair lightened; maybe that's why you don't recognize me."

"She was only seven when she saw you last," Iris snapped.

Monica put her arms around the tall, silent girl and hugged her. "My baby has grown up to be a beauty."

Brenda seemed to be stunned into silence. Her eyes appealed to her sister for help. "Iris? . . ."

"Brenda, baby. I know you're surprised to see me again. I would've called, but I wanted to make sure you'd be here when I got here." She smiled prettily

183

after darting a pointed glance at Iris, and fingered the ends of the hair that fell to Brenda's shoulders. "Come sit in the car and talk with me. I've come all the way from California to see you."

Iris moved rapidly to the screened door and flung it open. "You can talk to her in the house, if she wants to talk to you."

Brenda looked from one to the other, then turned and walked back inside. Monica followed, then Iris.

In the living room Brenda sank down on the couch, and Monica sat beside her. Iris stood hesitantly in the doorway.

"I'd like to spend some time with my daughter . . . alone," Monica said.

"That's up to Brenda," Iris responded icily.

Arthur came bounding into the room and ran to Brenda, his tail wagging so hard and so fast in his pleasure that his hind legs almost left the floor. John followed him at a much slower pace. Iris fastened her eyes on his face and failed to see the look that came over Monica's when she saw him. Iris did, however, hear her gasp, and turned to see her getting to her feet, her face wreathed in smiles.

"Johnny? Johnny Lang! Darling . . . what in the world are you doing here?"

John stopped, and his eyes narrowed. He put his hand to his lower lip and pulled on it. "I don't think—"

"Sure you do. Monica. Monica Ouverson. Oh, my God! It was at least thirteen or fourteen years ago. You were here on leave from the Navy. Visiting someone?

Was that it? We had a gorgeous time for a couple of weeks; then in San Diego—"

"I remember," John said slowly. "But I never connected you with this Ouverson family. The area is full of Ouversons."

By this time Monica had wrapped her arms around his neck and was kissing him. When Iris recovered from shock she was sure she was living out a nightmare. Her heart screamed for her not to listen to the logic that pounded in her mind. *John was the serviceman Monica had run away with!* The cold lump that was Iris's heart beat slowly. Icy fingers ran along her jaw, and she clenched her teeth to keep her face from crumpling.

"Do you live here, Johnny?" Monica seemed to have forgotton there was anyone else in the room.

"Not with us. He lives in the trailer on his half of the farm." The words tumbled like chips of ice from Iris's stiff lips.

"You live here on the farm?" Monica's tinkling laugh added more fuel to the rage that was beginning to smolder in Iris.

"What's so funny about that?" John asked quietly.

"Nothing, darling. I just can't imagine you, of all people, living *here.*"

"Get out!" The words burst from Iris. "I don't have to stand here and listen to your derogatory references to my home!"

"Darling . . ." Monica purred, ignoring Iris's outburst and looking up into John's face. "I'm sorry if

185

I've ruffled Iris's feathers. I want to spend some time with my daughter. I'd like her to meet my husband. We've come all the way from California just so he can meet her. Iris has some insane notion that I'm a monster, or something."

John looked over her head to Iris. She gazed steadily back at him, her eyes wide and hostile. "That's up to Iris and Brenda." He moved out of the reach of Monica's clinging hands. "Brenda?" His voice seemed to jar the girl, and she got to her feet. "Do you want to spend some time with your mother?"

"Who in the hell do you think you are?" Iris shouted. "Stay out of this!" Tight bands of tension were beginning to squeeze her head.

"Calm down, Iris. Brenda is old enough to make the decision for herself. She should spend a few hours with Monica if she wants to. The choice should be hers."

"Damn you! I don't need advice from . . . *you!*"

"Iris . . . don't." Tears stood in Brenda's eyes.

"Do you want to go?" Iris demanded.

"I . . . don't know."

John moved over and put his arm across Iris's shoulders. Iris moved out from under it and across the room to her sister. "Don't let him pressure you into going if you don't want to go," Iris said desperately.

"Oh, for heaven's sake! You'd think I wanted to take her on a trip around the world instead of just down the highway to the motel. My God! I'm her mother! I won't let any harm come to her."

"Some mother," Iris sneered.

186

"Iris, don't make it hard for Brenda." John was beside her. "Let her go. Let her use the common sense we both know she has." When Iris didn't look at him, or speak, he turned to Monica. "What motel and what name are you using?"

"My husband's name. Randolph. He's well known in real estate on the West Coast. Here's his card." She dug into her shoulder bag and handed him a business card.

"What are you going to do, Brenda?"

"Do you think I should go, John?"

Iris felt as if the earth were slipping out from under her. Suddenly John's wishes were more important to Brenda than hers.

"If you want to, kid," he was saying. "Someday you may want to know about the woman who birthed you. Giving birth to you and being a mother to you are two different things. If you remember, we've discussed that before."

"I think I'll go. If Iris . . ."

Iris clamped her lips together and willed the tears to stay behind her eyes. She nodded and tried to smile into the young girl's pleading eyes, silently saying, I'm here and I love you.

Brenda followed Monica through the dining room and kitchen to the door. Iris stood as if frozen. John watched her for an instant, then strode through the rooms and out the door. Iris saw him talking to Monica while Brenda went around the car to get in on the other side.

The breakfast Iris had eaten so happily suddenly turned on her. Her stomach churned, and the pain on the top of her head knifed down between her eyes. Abruptly she was in a black, swirling mist. She stumbled to the stairs. Escape. Damn him! Damn the whole rotten world! Damn this pain in her head! In the bathroom she gulped down several pills with a sip of water and carried pills and water to her room.

Betrayed. Iris sank down on the bed and pulled the pillow over her head. An iron band was trying to crush her skull. Pain. She'd had more headaches since she'd met John Lang than she'd had during the last ten years. Headaches and heartaches. Peaks and valleys. Love and despair. Fate had really kicked her in the teeth this time. The man she loved had been her stepmother's lover.

She wept.

"Iris . . . sweetheart?"

She'd known he would come. There was no way she could have prevented it, so she hadn't tried. "Get out!" Her muffled voice came from beneath the pillow. "Get out of my room, my house, my life and . . ." my heart, she added silently.

"Did you take your pills?"

"Yes, I took the pills! Get the hell out of here! I don't need or want your sympathy."

"Don't worry about Brenda. Seeing Monica could be the best thing for her at this time in her life. She'll—"

Iris threw off the pillow and sat up. Her head was

being split by the pain and her eyes were seeing colors running together.

"You bastard! How dare you stand there and tell me, so piously, what's best for my sister?" Tears streamed from her eyes and glued wisps of hair to her cheeks. "You're the man her mother went away with! She left my father and a tiny baby for . . . you! Stay away from Brenda. Stay away from me. I've been ten times a fool, but no more! I finally see you for what you are! Ohhh . . ." She retched. It came without warning, spewed out of her mouth, down the side of the bed, and onto the floor. It was the final humiliation.

Iris fell back on the bed and pulled the pillow over her head once again. From the depths of her weariness, she heard the bedroom door close. Once. again she was alone in the private sanctuary of her room, safe from watching, critical eyes. She curled herself into a tight ball and surrendered to the overwhelming sense of loss that sent burning tears streaming down her face once again.

Later, exhausted, she slept.

She woke from a nightmare of a dream where she was wandering in a vast open plain looking for Brenda. Her sister was leaning over her.

"Are you okay?"

"Sure. I was having a dream."

"You called me. I've been sitting over there waiting for you to wake up. How's your head?"

"I don't know yet. I'm afraid to move it. Oh . . . watch it, honey. I threw up. It must be a mess."

"It's okay. John cleaned it up before I got back."

"Oh, God, no!" Iris groaned.

Brenda came around to sit on the bed. "Did my going with her cause the headache?"

"No. It was a combination of things. What time is it?"

"Almost eight o'clock. You slept a long time." Brenda climbed farther up on the bed and crossed her legs Indian fashion. "Are you hungry? Can I get you something?"

"A cup of tea sounds good, but I'll get it later."

"Can I tell you about . . . it?" Brenda questioned hesitantly. "I'm glad I went. But I could tell you didn't want me to go."

"Tell me only if you want to, honey. No, I didn't want you to go. I was afraid you'd be impressed with her glamour. And maybe I was just jealous. I don't know."

"That's funny, Iris. No one in the world could ever take your place. You and I are family."

Iris choked back tears. "Thanks for saying that, useless nuisance." She tried to bring some lightness to her voice, and failed miserably.

"I've been wondering about her. She's very beautiful. I can't imagine why she ever married our dad." Brenda's brows puckered into a frown. "Why'd she do it?"

Iris searched for words. "She must have thought she loved him. Her family was poor and Dad was lonely. He bought her pretty clothes and she was happy for a while."

"I'm glad you're not like her. She's pretty, but she gushes and she's not very smart or she wouldn't have married Mr. Randolph. I didn't like him. He's got fat hands."

Iris tried not to smile. "Is that the only reason you didn't like him?"

"No. He wheezes when he talks, and he smokes smelly cigars. I don't think he could bend over and tie his shoes," she said with distaste. "She fusses over him like he was a king or somethin'. Yuk! He wasn't even as tall as she was! On the way back she kept telling me how rich he was, and showed me her diamond. They've got a swimming pool . . ." Brenda's voice trailed off.

Iris held her breath for a long moment and waited.

"I'm glad I went with her, Iris. Now I don't have to wonder what she's like." Brenda lay down on the bed beside her and cuddled up to her as she had done when she was small. "Do you think I'll be like her?" she asked in a scared whisper. "I don't want to be like her!"

"Oh, honey!" Iris hugged her. Relief flooded her heart. "You'll be whatever you want to be. You won't be like me or Monica. You'll be you."

"But I've got her blood."

"Not only hers, but our dad's. Don't worry about it. You're sensible, beautiful, healthy, and smart! What more do you want, obnoxious brat?" she asked teasingly, and batted the tears from her eyes.

"I'll never, never leave you, Iris." Brenda's arm tightened and she hugged her desperately.

"Sure, you will. Do you think I want you hanging around here when you're fifty and I'm sixty-eight? You'll meet some nice man and fall head over tail gate in love with him. You'll build a home together and have babies . . . to bring back home."

"Iris. John told me not to talk to you about this, but—"

"Then, don't." The words came out sharper than she had intended, and she was afraid she had broken the fragile thread of communication between them.

"I want to tell you," she said stubbornly. "John didn't know Monica was married. He didn't know she was going to follow him back to San Diego."

"I don't want to hear about it, Brenda. That's his business and hers."

"I wished you liked him more. He likes you. I can tell. We've had some good talks together. He talks to me as if he thinks what I have to say is important. I've never known anyone like him."

"That's nice," Iris said aloud, then added silently, You haven't known many men, punkin'. He's had twenty years' training in winning young minds over to his way of thinking. Quietly, she said, "I won't tell you not to be friends with him, but leave me out of it. I can never be friends with John Lang."

—Or his lover, her heart cried silently.

Twelve

"Absolutely not! You're making me angry, Brenda. You cannot ask him to eat with us tonight, or any night!"

"But Iris—"

"Don't argue." Iris yanked off her straw hat and wiped her forehead on the sleeve of her shirt. "I'm sorry, honey. I'm tired. I've got to get the rest of the garden in before . . . Arthur! Get him out of here, Brenda. He's digging up the cucumber seeds!"

"Oh, awright. C'mon, Arthur, or I'll tie you up."

Since Monica's visit Iris had worked like a demon in order to keep her sanity. School was out. Brenda did most of the household chores, leaving Iris free to work in the vegetable garden. The girl had been strangely subdued since the meeting with her mother. She hadn't mentioned her since the first night, which added to Iris's unease. That, and the fact that she was spending a lot of time with John.

Iris started the tiller as soon as Brenda left with the dog. Her arms ached from holding onto the heavy machine that chewed the soil, but that was nothing compared to the pain in her heart. She would get over it, she assured herself. It would take longer, since she had to see him every day, hear his voice, know he was near.

John had made an attempt to talk to her the day after Monica's visit, and she had stopped him cold.

"I may have to tolerate you here on the farm, Mr. Lang, but I don't have to tolerate your meddling in my private life. Butt out!"

He'd pushed his billed cap to the back of his head and glared at her. "You stubborn little jackass! You think everything is either black or white, and there are no shades of gray at all. You love me, dammit! You told me so a hundred times that night! You enjoyed our lovemaking as much as I did." Iris's face had flamed at that. "We could build a good life here together if it weren't for your damned stubborn pride. I'll tell you this once again, for the last time. I didn't know Monica was married to your father. I didn't know she had a child. I didn't ask her to follow me to California. You can believe whatever you want to believe. I've made my last move. Now it's up to you."

"It'll be a cold day in hell before I come to you for any reason at all!"

"We'll see about that," he said with a snarl, and walked away from her.

Now they were at loggerheads, and Brenda was torn between them.

Iris knelt to separate the spindly tomato plants. She was so deep in thought that she was startled when Brenda hunkered down beside her.

"John took Arthur with him, so I didn't have to tie him up. He took the pickup over to Alvin's to get some feed. He says we'll have to put up another building soon. He says it's too much to ask Alvin to store stuff for us. John says he's going to have a talk with you about making the farm a corporation. I'd be an officer, too." Brenda was smiling broadly. "Won't that be funny? Me, Brenda Ouverson, chairman of the board."

"I doubt you'd be chairman, honey. *He'd,* more than likely, reserve that position for himself."

Her sarcasm was lost on her sister. "Oh, that's okay. I just wish . . . you liked him more." The phrase was becoming a familiar one.

"We can't all like the same things, or the same people, can we?" Iris tried to be patient. "Will you pour some water from the bucket in the holes I dug along the fence?"

Brenda got up. "John says he'll run a water pipe along the top of the ground so you won't have to drag that heavy hose all the way out here to water the garden, if you want him to."

"Brenda, please don't say, 'John says,' another time today. Do that for me, will you, honey?" Her words sobered her sister, and Iris felt a stab of guilt.

"You're like a cow with a sore tail," Brenda muttered.

"So? Well, this *cow* has work to do." Iris pretended to be absorbed in the planting so her sister wouldn't see the tears in her eyes.

"*He* asked me to ride into town with him after lunch," Brenda said stubbornly. "I don't suppose you want me to go with *him.*"

"Go if you want to." Her voice was strained, her throat constricted with the jealousy she could not dis-

195

miss from her mind. She tried to hide it with a rebuke. "How many times have I told you not to take a negative attitude when you want something?"

"Cripes! I never know what kind of attitude to take with you anymore. You're always so cross."

"I'm sorry," Iris murmured, and plunged her hands down into the soft mud surrounding the plant.

Brenda and John didn't return from town until dinner time. Iris was standing at the kitchen sink, looking out over the yard, when the pickup came up the drive. Arthur was riding proudly in the truck bed amid sacks of feed. Brenda jumped from the truck the instant it stopped, and made for the house. John caught the back of her T-shirt and stopped her.

"Oh, no, you don't. The deal was that you'd help unload. So get to it. Take the bridles and the small stuff to the shed while I unload the feed."

Their voices and laughter drifted into the kitchen. With aching despair Iris walked slowly into the living room and turned on the television set to watch the evening news. There had been a mud slide in California, a flood in Mississippi, and a tornado in Oklahoma. The whole world seemed to reflect her mood. She turned off the set and waited in the quiet for her sister to come in.

The next afternoon Iris straightened her aching back and wondered why she had enlarged the garden. She and Brenda would never use all the fruits of her efforts. Two dozen tomato plants? And then squash, green peppers, peas, beans and even eggplant. Oh, lordy! What would she do with six bushels of beets? She took off her gloves and dug her hand into her jeans pocket for a tissue. While wiping her brow she walked to the strawberry bed. In another week, she mused, she'd be crawling between the rows picking berries.

"Iris! I-r-is!" Brenda's scream jerked her out of her musings. "Iris!" The frantic note in her voice caused Iris's heart to stop, then speed ahead in alarm. Sugar was coming up the lane from the field at full gallop, with Brenda clinging to her back. The colt ran behind trying to keep up. "John . . . John . . . John . . ." she gasped, and then wailed, "Ohhh . . ."

Iris grabbed the bridle to hold the excited horse still. "Calm down! Tell me!"

"He fell off the tractor and there's . . . there's blood!" she screeched.

"Oh, God, no! Call an ambulance!" The full impact of her sister's words hit Iris like a blow between the eyes.

"Help him! It'll be too late!" she wailed. She held out her hand. Iris took it and leaped up behind her.

Sugar took off on the run. Iris had to reach around her sister and grab the horse's mane to keep from sliding off the rump. Her hand encountered something damp and red on Brenda's jeans. Blood! Oh, dear God, don't let this be happening! Please don't let him be hurt, be . . . dead. She was almost petrified with fear. Her knees were so weak she could barely clamp them to the heaving sides of the running horse.

At the far end of the field she could see the big green tractor with the six-row cultivator attached. Her eyes clung to the machine and searched the ground as they came closer. Unaware that her respiration was coming in short, labored gasps, his name pounded in her mind with every beat of her heart. John . . . John . . . John . . .

Brenda pulled the horse up so short the animal almost reared. Iris slid off and stumbled to where John lay on the ground, his body against the sharp tines of the cultivator. Blood-red wetness covered his chest.

"Call an ambulance," she screamed at Brenda. "Tell them to hurry." She wasn't aware when her sister put her heels to the horse and raced away.

Her chest contracted with pain. It was as if someone were cutting her with a hot knife. "John . . . darling, darling . . ."

She fell on her knees beside him and looked into his face. It was smeared with dirt, and a streak of dark red ran down his neck from the corner of his mouth.

"Please, please, be all right. Darling . . . be all right!" His shirt was soaked, and his arm lay beneath him. She slipped her hand beneath his head to turn his face toward her. His eyelashes fluttered and his lips twisted in pain. "Thank God you're alive! Sweetheart, darling, I know you can't hear me, but lie still. Brenda's gone to call the ambulance." I must stop the bleeding, she thought wildly. But with what?

She drew her hand from beneath his head. It was sticky and wet. Her breath almost left her. Quickly she unbuttoned her shirt and slipped out of it. She bent over him to unbutton his shirt, and the white cup of her bra dipped in the thick red ooze on his chest. Sobbing, she stuffed her wadded shirt into his.

"I've been such a stubborn fool, darling." Tears ran down her face. "I love you. Please don't die. Live, so I can tell you how much I love you and how much I want to marry you . . . live with you . . . have your babies . . ."

A groan came from deep in his throat. Iris held his face in her hands and bent to kiss his lips. Arthur nudged against her. "Get away," she said frantically. Arthur backed off a few steps and looked at her. She turned back to John and stroked his cheek with a feathery touch. "Hold on, darling . . . help is coming," she crooned.

Arthur jumped over John's legs to reach the other side. To her horror he began to lick John's neck.

"You beast! You contemptible beast! Get away from him or I'll kill you!" Iris shouted between sobs, and tried to hit him with her hat.

Arthur backed off, cocked his head to one side, and looked at her.

John muttered and moaned.

"What is it, darling? Just lie still."

He muttered again, and she bent her head so her ear was against his lips.

"Kiss . . . me . . ." The words were barely a whisper.

"Kiss you? Yes, darling." She placed her lips gently to the side of his mouth.

Arthur's thick body pushed against her. The beast was licking again! This time it was John's shirt. Iris hit at him again. John muttered, and she placed her face close to his so she could hear him.

"What is it, sweetheart?"

"I said, I accept." His voice boomed in her ear. She jerked her head back and found herself looking into bright, twinkling blue eyes.

"What . . . did you say?" Iris felt her mouth go slack.

"I said, I'll marry you. Tomorrow. Thanks for asking me." His arms snaked out, grabbed her, and crushed her to him. He rolled over and pinned her to the ground before she could catch her breath.

Blood pounded in her ears, and her vision blurred red. She teetered between reality and unconsciousness. The mouth that ground into hers had the taste of . . . smelled like . . . *catsup!* A ringing from far, far away filled her ears. John lifted his mouth. His face was all she could see. It was smiling! Reality and rage washed over her like a thundershower.

"You . . ." she sputtered. "You . . . "

Using strength she didn't know she possessed she pushed him off her and scrambled to her feet, His hand shot out and grabbed her ankle. She kicked at him with her other foot, and his steel grip tightened around her leg. Her rump hit the soft ground, and her hand landed on her straw hat. It was the only weapon available. She began to flay him with it.

"Take that . . . and that . . . you beast, worm, slimy toad . . . you miserable redheaded woodpecker! You're

200

despicable, rotten, evil! If I were a man I'd beat you to death!"

"If you were a man, sweetheart, I wouldn't be so wild to marry you. Brenda! Get that hat away from her before she puts my eyes out!"

Brenda came from the other side of the tractor. "What's the matter, Junior? Can't you handle her? I did my part."

"Get the hat, dammit, before she beats me to death." John was trying to dodge the blows. "Cripes! That catsup has run down into my pants. You overdid it, brat."

"What are ya complaining about? It worked."

"Arthur thought I was a hot dog."

"Next time we'll use barbecue sauce. He doesn't like it." Brenda snatched the battered, smeared hat from her sister's hand. "Why'd ya take your shirt off? You've got catsup all over your bra, Iris. Cripes! You look funny! You've got it in your hair, too."

"You two planned this . . . joke. I hope you got your money's worth," Iris said shakily, her voice beginning to break.

"Get lost, kid," John said gently. "You've done your part. Now it's all up to me."

"It's about time. I was thinkin' I'd have to propose for you." Brenda had a look of disgust on her young face. "C'mon, Arthur, 'n' stop drooling."

"I don't have to propose. She already asked me and I accepted." His smile was anxious as he moved closer to Iris. She looked as if she would burst into tears any minute.

"Holy purple pot roast!" Brenda's face broke into a beautiful smile, and she jumped up in the air and clicked her scuffed sneakers together. "I'm a better actress than I thought I was. Superneat! Double superneat!" She threw her arms around her sister and kissed her. "Yuk!" She backed off. "That catsup is messy. Maybe we should've used tomato juice." She ran to the horse. "C'mon. Let's leave the lovers alone. Whoopee!" she shouted, and turned the horse in a circle before she raced away.

As if all this were happening to someone else, Iris watched her sister. Her eyes swung back to John, and they looked at each other for a long moment. His fingers were hooked in the waistband of her jeans, and his leg was thrown over hers, as if he expected her to scramble to her feet and run. He smiled at her quietly.

"Hi," he said softly. "Did you know you're sitting in the middle of a plowed field without a shirt, and you've got catsup on your bra?"

"You . . . fight dirty."

"I know. But I was desperate. Brenda came up with the idea." She saw pleading in his eyes. He wasn't as sure of himself as he wanted her to believe.

"You scared the hell out of me."

"I'm sorry." The words didn't go with the idiotic smile on his face. "I was sure you loved me. We had to figure out a way to make you break out of your shell and admit it." She looked at him blankly. "Do

202

you want your shirt back?" He pulled it out of the front of his. It was stained, but he managed to find a clean spot and wiped her face. He removed his own shirt and tried to wipe some of the catsup off his chest.

"I don't know if I'll be able to take you and Brenda together," she said in a broken voice. The sobs were very near.

"A desperate situation called for desperate action, sweetheart. Are we forgiven?" He pushed her back into the soft earth and saw the tears run from the corners of her eyes.

"You . . . crazy idiots! I could've had a heart attack. It would've served you right, too!"

"You're not getting another headache?" he asked anxiously, and leaned over her to rest on his forearms, his thumbs on her temples to wipe at the tears.

"I don't think so. I've had enough headaches the last few months to last a lifetime." She wanted to bury her face against his neck and cry with relief.

"I'll do my best not to give you any more headaches. I love you." His lips moved across her face, found her nose, then her lips. He kissed her gently and lovingly. "I've been waiting weeks for that. Hum . . . mm, you taste good. Like a French-fried potato." His blue eyes held hers. "Put your arms around me."

"We shouldn't . . ." she whispered as she obediently wound her arms about his neck.

"No one can see us but the birds, and they're only interested in other birds."

"You're crazy, but I love you."

Their lips moved together. "Sweetheart . . . love . . ." He whispered love words softly, and his mouth moved over her face to meet her lips again and again, hard and demanding at first, then tenderly as his tongue moved to part her lips and taste the sweetness of her mouth.

"Talk to me, babe. Tell me everything that's happened in your life, and I'll tell you about mine. Darling, about Monica—"

She placed her fingers over his lips. "No. I remember how she was. I know what you told me was true. I just didn't want to believe it at the time. The hurt was too new."

"After we're married, I want to adopt Brenda. I've given it a lot of thought. I want to be more than a brother-in-law. I really love that kid."

For a few minutes Iris was swamped with emotion. She managed a shaky smile when she saw the anxiety in his eyes.

"Are you sure?"

"Absolutely. I'd like a boy, too. Wanta make one?"

"Here? Now?" She laughed and squirmed against him. Her taut nipples in the wet bra raked across his chest.

"He'd be a unique kid. Kids at school would say, 'Hey, Sam. Where were you conceived?' He'd say, 'Out in the cornfield one warm June day. My folks were stuck together with catsup at the time.'"

"Mister, you've lost a few bricks!" Laughter bubbled from her lips and danced in her smoky eyes.

"I love to hear you laugh." His voice was abruptly

husky. "Promise me you'll laugh every day for the next fifty years."

"Make it forty and it's a deal." Her eyes remained brilliant with laughter and love. His face was a mixture of astonishment and delight. He pinched her bottom. "Yeoo . . ." She choked off the yelp of surprise and tickled his ribs.

They rolled in the dirt and laughed. Then he kissed her long and hard while running his hands down her slender form. The bra was pushed aside, and the jeans, which kept his hands from her soft skin, were loosened. They lay entwined, not making love, content to be there together. There was plenty of time.

John lifted his head, and his eyes held hers in mischievous bondage. Her eyes shone up into his, and her mouth couldn't keep from smiling. It was so very magical to be held close, with his arms locked around her, her tired body resting against his—their minds attuned.

"If the neighbors saw me lying in the dirt with you they'd think I'd flipped out, for sure."

"Yeah. I can hear 'em. Strange things goin' on over at the Ouverson place, they'd say. It should liven up the talk at the feed store."

"At the Lang place," she corrected gently.

He smiled and kissed her nose. His eyes glittered happily, and his fingers worried her nipple, gently exciting her. "I can't believe my luck, wanton woman. I love you very much and in many ways I didn't know a man could love a woman. I fell in love right away and nearly cried when you hated me so much." The smile in his eyes and on his lips was real. His hand moved over her body in what seemed a reverent way.

Iris wound her arms around his neck and pressed closer to him. She knew she was loved and that she loved in return. He knew it, too. She could tell by the unfettered look of pleasure in his eyes when he gazed at her. This was home—the safest, most wonderful place in all the world. It would still be home if they were on a Pacific island or in an Alaskan igloo. This long, lean body pressed to hers was the torch that lighted her life.

Iris felt hot breath on her face and dreamily opened her eyes. Arthur's nose was inches away. His head was cocked to one side, and his tongue lolled.

"Arthur! You're drooling." Laughter rippled in John's voice. He rolled her over him and away from the dog. He kissed her face and nibbled on her neck, biting softly and sucking gently. "Do you like that, sweetheart?"

"Uh-huh."

"Can't you be a little bit more enthusiastic?" he asked with a growl.

"Well . . ." Her eyes glinted down at him as she pondered the question. "They're better kisses than I'd get from Arthur."

Her peals of laughter were cut off abruptly.

Center Point Publishing
600 Brooks Road • PO Box 1
Thorndike ME 04986-0001 USA

(207) 568-3717

US & Canada:
1 800 929-9108
www.centerpointlargeprint.com